A Long Walk to Purgatory

The Tales of Dante & Mashudu

Chariklia Martalas

UJ Press

A Long Walk to Purgatory

Published by UJ Press
University of Johannesburg
Library
Auckland Park Kingsway Campus
PO Box 524
Auckland Park
2006
https://ujonlinepress.uj.ac.za/

Compilation © Chariklia Martalas 2023
Chapters © Chariklia Martalas 2023
Published Edition © Chariklia Martalas 2023

First published 2023

https://doi.org/10.36615/9781776425686

978-1-7764256-7-9 (Paperback)
978-1-7764256-8-6 (PDF)
978-1-7764256-9-3 (EPUB)
978-1-7764341-0-7 (XML)

This publication had been submitted to a rigorous double-blind peer-review process prior to publication and all recommendations by the reviewers were considered and implemented before publication.

Copy editor: Kyleigh Greatorex
Cover design: Hester Roets, UJ Graphic Design Studio
Typeset in 10/13pt Merriweather Light

Contents

Synopsis

A Long Walk to Purgatory is a play that places Dante in the South African context. It works with the idea that dead poets must guide living poets through the afterlife on a journey of poetic reckoning. It is now Dante's turn to guide a poet, as he was once guided by Virgil. Dante comes to meet Mashudu, a South African poet in her Dark Wood. He comes to take her through Inferno and Purgatory where she meets South African characters along the way including Jan Van Riebeeck and John Dube. Driving the play is the notion that poets need to know where they come from in order to play their role as aids to how a nation understands itself. This means Mashudu has to witness the truth of her context both in terms of the narrative of South Africa as a country and her own personal morality. Mashudu, guided by Dante, reckons with her understanding of South Africa's past such as with witnessing the punishment of Verwoerd, to reckoning with the country's present including a domestic abuser. Mashudu is also faced with the precariousness of her own morality when she meets an old friend in Purgatory. As the play continues, Dante becomes Mashudu's friend showing that friendship can cross centuries and contexts for poets share their role as poets no matter the society to which they belong. Both Mashudu and Dante are connected by their unwavering commitment to their own moral imagination. Virgil, as comic relief, completes the picture as narrator, cementing the idea that the poets of the past are deeply connected to the poets of the present. Ultimately, *A Long Walk to Purgatory* aims to show the importance of literature to both be grounded in and transcend particularities of time and place. Literature can ultimately open up a new space for us that is both informed by a context but is intrinsically connected to a wider humanity.

Dedication

To my family, it has always been a dream to dedicate a piece of writing to you. Now that dream has come true.
Thank you for everything.

To the real Mashudu

And lastly... To Dante, my Beatrice

Part One: Inferno

Prologue

The stage is empty before the audience. It is stripped of any of those extravagances that can offer clues of the beginning that will soon uncoil itself. Like all beginnings and other beings of time, the beginning must be summoned. The audience needs to be brought into the folds of the new world they have given themselves to. The beginning shakes her limbs like the other beasts of Dante's Dark Wood. She shows us that the right way is to start where no right way can be found. The stage may be empty but the theatre will not be. Dante was a poet, so let it be words that let the Dark Wood grow from the ceilings and the seats. Beginnings have always been creatures with mouths filled with unformed phrases.

Entering the Dark Wood

The strangeness of Inferno has always been that the beauty of language is in opposition to the horror of its meaning. As the audience comes in they experience the beauty before its distortion. The first lines of Inferno are spoken in the original Italian, so Dante's poetry can be honoured. If this is where Dante began then so shall we. Dante's words are not recited, rather, they are sacredly chanted. It is almost as if the hum of the poetry is asking Dante to soon be part of the theatre space. It is an acknowledgement. We will begin with you Dante, the chant is saying. We will bring you close.

Nel mezzo del cammin di nostra vita mi ritrovai per una selva oscura che la diritta via era smarrita. Ah, quanto a dir qual era e cosa dura esta selvaggia e aspra e fortre che nel pensier rinova la paura! Tant'e amara che poco e più morte; ma per trattar del ben ch'io vi trovai diro dellaltre cose ch'i v'ho scorte. (1–10)

The Dark Wood is Growing

The Dark Wood is not just a place that Dante finds himself lost in. The Dark Wood is a state of mind. It is not only exile from the perfections of sanity. It is an untethering from what was known before. This comes with the demand of having to find a new way to be. The Dark Wood is a mind in pain, disorientated and held tightly by the unknown. In the Dark Wood, Dante felt the beginning unearth itself, and so should we. While the audience is settling in they must become unsettled. To be in the Dark Wood, the birth place of the beginning, is for the Dark Wood to inhabit one's mind.

The sacred hum of Inferno's opening lines is joined by its translations. However, the translations are not synchronised to their source. Rather, the translations almost perforate the lucidity of Dante's Italian text. The poetics are there but incongruous. The beauty is being pierced as if each translated line is a needle. What is important is that when the translations are introduced they are not spoken harshly but are instead also chanted. The alienation the voices wish to cause is a slow conquering. Strangeness is suggested before it overwhelms.

Nel mezzo del cammin di nostra vita

> Halfway along our journey to life's end

mi ritrovai per una selva oscura

che la diritta via era smarrita

> I found myself astray in a dark wood

Ah, quanto a dir qual era e cosa dura

> Since the right way was nowhere to be found

> How hard a thing it is to express the horror

esta selvaggia e aspra e fortre

> Of that wild wood, so difficult, so dense!

> Even to think of it renews my terror

che nel pensier rinova la paura!

Tant'e amara che poco e più morte;

ma per trattar del ben ch'io vi trovai

    It is so bitter death is scarcely more

diro dellaltre cose ch'I ho scorte

    But to convey what goodness I discovered

    I shall tell everything that I saw there

As the chant progresses more lines from Inferno Canto I and their translations are weaved in. The chant is spoken more harshly with sharp hisses and unlikely pauses. It has become uncomfortable and savage in its knife-toothed rhythm. The sacredness leaks out from the chant. Poetry is being mangled as the Dark Wood grows.

What is important is that there are a few lines that are repeated more regularly. These lines are repeated both with the English and Italian as well as other possible translations.

"Half way along our journey to life's end"

"I found myself astray in a dark wood"

"Since the right way is nowhere to be found"

The line repeated most often is:

"I shall tell everything that I saw there."

Subsumed by the Dark Wood

The theatre lights are extinguished and the audience is dropped into a thick and reaching darkness.

The savageness of the voices becomes married to the sounds of the beasts. They are not animal-like because they bring an unnatural horror. Their monstrous growls and snarls are both metallic and human. They are other than what is natural because the Dark Wood is a human creation. Dante's descriptions of the leopard, the lion and the wolf claw themselves into the sacrilegious chant. The words of Dante's poetry is screamed and shouted, spitted and choked. The poetry is spoken like a curse that engulfs the theatre completely. It rages from the centre and the edges so the audience cannot know the direction of its true origin. The Dark Wood has overpowered and tortured Dante's words. It is an exile from beauty, it is an exile from knowing where to turn.

Nel mezzo del cammin di nostra vita (GROWL)

(GROWL)   *Questi parea che contra me venisse*

Halfway along our journey to life's end

The pain she caused me was so terrible (GROWL)

mi ritrovai per una selva oscura

And such the terror coming from her sight

Nel mezzo del cammin di nostra vita

(GROWL) With head held high, and so irate with hunger

si volse a retro a rimirar lo passo

I shall tell everything that I saw there (GROWL)

(GROWL) It did seem that the beast was drawing near

che la diritta via era smarrita

Though it had filled my heart to overflowing

mi ritrovai per una selva oscura

che non lascio già mai persona viva

che la diritta via era smarrita. (GROWL)

cosi l'animo mio ch'ancor fuggiva

I found myself astray in a dark wood (GROWL)...

The sacrilegious chant ends abruptly. The Dark Wood has decided there is another way to reign. The voices were oppressive and forceful in their presence. The Dark Wood was too full, the discomfort pressed against the skin of the audience and the gaps between the seats were stacked with deformed sounds heavy as stones. Now, there is an oppressive silence. The Dark Wood can punish in being everything and nothing. The silence weaves its way between the legs of the audience like smoke. Yet, there is hope for the emptiness feels untrue. The beginning is uncoiling its tight limbs as the stage lightens. Out of the silence forms the jagged shapes of the Dark Wood. There, in the corner, is the bold outline of a young woman. The beginning has taken its first breath.

Scene I

Inferno Canto I

The silence is sharp. The revealed stage brings with it a lucidity as thin as a blade. Now the Dark Wood can be recognised, though the voices have not resurrected. The audience sees a stage that is lit with shadows. Bodies of darkness fight against small wisps of light, allowing the audience to trace the skeleton of an entangled forest. There is a brutality to the jagged branches that reach to the limits and turn back on themselves. It can make anyone melancholic just to see how the ribbons of shadow tie themselves in patterns. There is no sense of the wood ending or any hope in the belief that the sky is close or that the edges can be touched. The claustrophobic bodies of the trees are mocking. They tell the audience that they have been captured by the shaded smoke. Their eyes have been kidnapped.

The audience is not alone. Mashudu walks across the stage leaving behind her trail of hesitations. She twists her whole body when she constantly looks behind her. Scared to find someone but scared to be alone. The tightness of the silence will not allow another sound through its teeth. Her loneliness needs to be tended to as she moves with uncertain limbs— every move a calculation but yet there is no right answer. So she walks not only with the desperation to be found but also to escape an anxious paralysis that leaves the endings and beginnings of her movements sudden, sharp and precarious. The Dark Wood breaks her shadow as it transforms its skeleton trees into a cage.

A new voice then announces itself from the audience as if it suddenly remembered it has a part to play. Virgil excuses himself as he tries to get onto the stage. Mouthing apologies and yet his curses are loud. His hands are both defensive and apologetic as he holds them out in front of him while making his way onto the stage. Virgil trips up the stairs in his haste to give himself a view of the audience, his body constantly looks off centre and restless. He is dressed in white with wreaths in his hair and pats his torso all over to finally find his box of Marlboro Reds. He blatantly looks out of place as he lights the cigarette, though he does not actually mind for he neither belongs to the story nor to the audience. Virgil is a man floating, suspended in **limbo** *wherever he goes.*

VIRGIL: More than 700 years ago, I saw a lost soul just like this one. He was a bit older and much uglier but lost nonetheless. So, kind as I am, doing the duty of a good pagan soul, I took the man Dante under my wing and led him through the afterlife. I am not here to tell you of that journey, you can read it yourself, though some translations I am told should be avoided. Actually, maybe all translations but sadly we can't all read Italian. Instead, I am here to watch another story, a story that is not a sequel like one of those movie franchises that don't have the art of the epic or the courtesy to end. Think of this as a continuation where Dante, my ingénue, can now take a soul through the afterlife on a pilgrimage of sorts and learn what it means to be a poetic guide. So who is this soul? Who is the soul that is lost and wandering in the Dark Wood? Her name is Mashudu, an ordinary South African woman who is filled with the idiosyncrasies of being young such as not liking Simba's salt and vinegar chips and feeling old when she can't stay out past midnight anymore no matter how fun the night is. And now she is lost, confused, with all the turmoil of a mind that doesn't know the right direction; which means of course Mashudu is a poet. Trust a poet to get herself in such a situation and trust it has to be a poet to get her out of it. Poetry is fundamentally a ridiculous occupation for anyone wishing to be sane. But I guess someone has to write those cultural relics that become trivia game questions, food for literature majors to eat upon and plays for audiences as good as this one. She is in line to inherit this purpose but unlike others she has the potential to do it well. Will you watch with me? Will you watch the pilgrimage unravel like a thread of fate? I see Dante walking into the forest. Can you see my nostalgia overflowing?

Mashudu will mirror the first lines of Inferno but with words that belong to her. Mashudu's fate is interwoven with Dante. She is a poet and a pilgrim, lost in the darkness of a mind in exile, a reflection of Dante himself when he was halfway to the journey of his life's end. But it is because Mashudu is a poet that she needs words of her own. She is not playing Dante, she is playing herself.

MASHUDU: (*looks straight at the audience*) I am halfway to somewhere, yet I don't know how to move forward. My mind feels like a forest with trees made from moving shadows. Those trees are sharp like razors. Why do they not leave me? Why can't I seem to leave them? The right way was lost ages ago, or I never knew it to begin with. I don't know how to tell you about how frightened I am. To tell you is to think of it and I cannot think of it for I am tired.

Dante comes into view, he is a bit awkward, but still determined while he looks around the Dark Wood. Mashudu must now decide what she fears most— another human or the loneliness. As a woman, she knows that a strange man is never a good bargain when wanting to escape isolation. Dante recognises her and begins walking towards her, his body is rigid with purpose but with no smile. Mashudu is alarmed at the directness but still allows herself to look at him with her shoulders on edge. Yet her whole body softens when she recognises something familiar in him or at the very least senses the possibility of friendship.

DANTE: I recognise your words though I had spoken them differently. I too am a poet. I sang the good.

MASHUDU: It is you Dante, isn't it? I couldn't see you so far away because of the damn shadows. I can finally see you clearly now.

She is curious but still hesitates before she asks. She knows that her fate caught her after so many years of wandering.

MASHUDU: Why are you here in South Africa? It has been so long after you died, I assumed it was for good. Who have you come to meet?

DANTE: (*his whole body straightens, as if dictating a manifesto*) I have been summoned to be your guide.

MASHUDU: You have come to meet me?

Dante gives her a stare to not interrupt and stands up even straighter. He has definitely rehearsed this since he starts again from scratch. It is with a kind of pride but also with a kind of nervousness.

DANTE: I have been summoned to be your guide, a divine mission I had to accept as one had accepted for me. Souls of virtue have sent me to take you on this perilous journey but you shall come to meet them without me. They will gaze upon you with heavenly light and there will be radiance as magnificent as the planet's rays, which "always guides all men and guides them right" (18). (*pauses*) You must follow me and take a different road. Are you not Mashudu?

MASHUDU: Yes I am but...

DANTE: Are you not a poet?

MASHUDU: I am attempting to be one.

Dante is cloaked in impatience, his body framed in sharp angles. Was he not more accepting when he was in this Dark Wood? Did he not put faith in Virgil, why is Mashudu not putting faith in him? What Dante does not realise is that he is asking—where is her ego? Dante hasn't encountered modern scepticism or at the very least he has forgotten the unease of being young. Mashudu is wary of being all-talk, she brings with her the rampant self-doubt of the best of her generation. Yet Dante says the lines he must say, though hiding behind them is the bite of a teacher who doesn't yet know how to teach.

DANTE: "I therefore think and judge it would be best// For you to follow me. And I shall lead// You to a region that will always last.// Where you will hear shrieks of despair and grief// And see the ancient spirits in their pain// As each of them begs for their second death// And you'll see spirits happy in the fire//

Because they live in hope that they will come// Sooner or later, where the blessed are." (112–120)

MASHUDU: I need to escape this Dark Wood. I feel it closing in. Dante, I have decided I will come with you. I know that you have left a place like this before. Though I have to be honest about how strange this is. Not a strangeness that is dark. It is something else, but I don't know what. I want to ask— why me? But I know for some odd reason this is not a mistake. Dante am I ready to go through the afterlife?

DANTE: You will meet those that God wishes you to know. We must find the souls whose fates need to be understood.

MASHUDU: (*she takes a step back, her shoulders leading her*) I am not ready...can anyone be ready for this?

Scene II

Inferno Canto III

Mashudu and Dante stand in front of the gates of Inferno. Mashudu begins to move backwards, each step more hurried until Dante pulls her back. He taps her shoulders and Mashudu then stands straight and strong in response.

But there is a reason Mashudu's body has attempted to falter. The gate feels like a precipice. It is a kind of chasm unto itself, as it stands formidable with its outstretched arms. Where the Dark Wood grew from the minds of humans exiled from sanity, the gate is imposed by an entity without any fragility. The gate is forged by the will of God, it has the marking of a righteous tyranny. An abyss now stands between freedom and punishment. Divine will has inscribed the duties of an eternal prison and so it must be that divine will protects Mashudu and Dante since they will be able to move through Inferno unchained. The gates will open onto something too great to be described. Inferno can only be felt.

DANTE: Will you read the inscription transcribed on the barrier between us and Inferno?

MASHUDU: I am scared to say Inferno out loud.

DANTE: To enter is to know where you are entering. We must begin right.

Inferno cracks open as Mashudu reads the words written on the gates. Her face is illuminated by great strikes of lightening and the thunder endlessly rumbles its delusional murmurings. As she speaks she hears snarls, growls and hisses. The whole stage shakes with a kind of beat as the feet of the damned bang on the floor and violently slap their hands. Wild bursts of maniacal laughter strike with the lightning. Whatever is behind the gates is jeering her as she recites God's words.

Yet Mashudu grows taller with every line as if divine will has entered her, her spine pulled up by God's words.

MASHUDU: "You go through me to a city of lamentation// You go through me to everlasting pain// You go through me to the forsaken nation// Justice inspired my maker up above// I was established by omnipotence// The highest wisdom and the primal love// Nothing before me was created ever// But everlasting things. And I shall last.// Abandon hope entirely, you who enter." (1-9)

The taunts of Inferno give way to the sounds of its pain. Inferno does not have the humanness of the Dark Wood for there is no distorted poetry or recognisable words. The pain is too great to form phrases, the punishment too deep to be coherent. The sounds that rise from the belly of Inferno are shrieks, unintelligible curses, screams and wails. The desperate mumblings are spoken with gibberish tongues that are ripped out of the mouths of the punished. The sounds become more chaotic as they deafen the theatre.

DANTE: We can only enter once you have told me honestly whether you have let your hope fall out of you. We will begin when you can hold your courage. Misgivings and doubts must die. Your spine must harden since we will move as hostages through the realm of everlasting sorrow. Though, you must not pity those who have been mangled by suffering. Never forget why they are there.

MASHUDU: (*checks her pulse, closes her eyes and takes a breath*) I am ready... I think. Dante were you ready? Because I think I am ready. I have known enough sadnesses. I am used to what is unhinged. But... Dante, tell me, were you ready? Let me stop asking this I am ready. I know, I know...don't look at me like that. I am ready, I promise. (*she begins walking with determination*) Let us go.

They walk through the gate into a wall of sound. The magnitude of Inferno can now wrap its cloak around them.

DANTE: "From this point, sighs, laments, and piercing groans// Were echoing throughout the starless air// Hearing them this first time, I wept at once// Deformed and diverse tongues, terrible sounds.// Words venting misery, outbursts of rage// Loud voices, soft ones, sounds of slapping hands// Combined into a turmoil always swirling// Throughout that unrelieved black atmosphere// Like sand which rises at a whirlwind's whirling.// (22–30)

MASHUDU: (*pausing to recoil*) The chaos feels painful, Dante. Who are these voices?

Dante just stretches his arms in front of him like a command. He gestures for Mashudu to keep walking. She looks at him and nods and then moves forward hurriedly despite looking back to see if Dante is really joining her.

Virgil laughs from the aisles. He is loose and flamboyant since he is finally not so flustered. The audience now remembers that the stage is not the only reality.

VIRGIL: Would you believe it if I told you I lived past those gates? Not the most prime real estate of the afterlife I can tell you that much. Trust me, a good pagan soul knows very well that house buying mantra— location, location, location. Pity I could not do it successfully. Let me say that being part of the Before Christ Club is not that great in the afterlife. Seriously, what could I have done when divine justice was my real estate agent?

Scene III

Inferno Canto V

Stretching out like a winding horizon, there is a queue to end all queues. Inferno has never found itself wanting for sinners and so the queue has never found a moment to shorten its reach. It was best measured in days rather than kilometres and best measured in years rather than days. The souls smothered in the crowd, are in competition for air. Soul upon soul, are crushed. It doesn't matter much now that they are dead, they cannot die again. They can only wait as they are eaten by the queue's serpentine body. The souls can only dislodge their limbs before judgement, until then, they are one with the rest of the damned. Waiting is one big grand emotion— an electric charge of nervousness that runs through every soul. It even reaches the two pilgrims standing at the tail of the snake. There are no silent prayers. It is too late for that. Not even a prayer for an easy punishment. What is done is done the rest is futile. What is left is only the waves of chattered teeth, the fear squeezing itself out of their eyes and the monotony of constant quivering hands.

Mashudu hums with a restrained excitement, despite the queue. Dante is calm but stiff.

MASHUDU: How will I know when I see Minos?

DANTE: "Minos is there, most horribly and grinding// His teeth. He judges guilt as people enter// And places them according to his winding// I mean that when the spirit born for ill// Comes in his sight, it makes a full confession// And then that expert on all sin can tell// What depth of Hell is most appropriate// Winding his long tail round himself to number// How many circles down it must be put.// Always there are large crowds. Each one in turn// Must stand in front of him to hear his judgement// They speak, they hear, they're straight away sent down." (4-15)

They shuffle forward. Mashudu itches closer to Dante with no subtlety.

MASHUDU: (*politely*) Listen, Dante, I am all for being polite when it comes to waiting. I had strict parents and all that. But it seems to me that since we are not damned, can we just not go ahead? The queue is longer than the ones at home. (*jokingly*) Or did you lure me to make a confession?

DANTE: A confession is not your fate, which I am sure will disgruntle Minos and his cattle teeth. (*looks ahead and squints*) There are so many more souls than I remember. These few centuries that have passed by show me how human souls have not been kind to history. (*pauses*) Impatience is not a virtue but this time you are right. Time holds us in her grip, I feel her pressing tighter.

Dante then points his arm forward like a needle on a compass— both straight and direct. Mashudu follows closely behind Dante, scared of being swallowed, but instead the souls open up the queue like the Red Sea parting. The serpent splits and unites as the pilgrims walk through. Yet Dante stops a few souls to the front and uses his arm to block Mashudu before she mindlessly hurtles into the next souls. Dante wants her to see the act of damnation being willed and enacted.

Once seeing Minos, Mashudu nearly laughs. She was expecting a gavel not a stapler and a pulpit not a desk with metal filing cabinets behind it. An oddly formed pot plant is sitting on one of the cabinets, the desk is dusted with papers and a mug is filled with something black and thick. Minos is standing with his dishevelled suit, slightly hunched. He is in a loose tie that becomes looser every time he tries to click his neck. He looks exhausted as black ink coats his hands and dark rings stick to the bottom of his Saturn-like eyes.

The hum of Mashudu's body is now louder, her hands almost try to grab Dante's cloak before she stops herself. Dante is slightly turned away from her, concentrating on what is ahead of them.

MASHUDU: Isn't it strange that Minos has a tie? Don't get me started that Inferno has paperclips.

DANTE: A tie?

MASHUDU: That thing around his neck. Look it is even striped. Minos' tie and these long queues make me feel that Hell is the bureaucratic nightmare we all said it would be. Does this not remind me of the time I had to get my passport renewed at Home Affairs? Time leaks out of your watch at those places. You've stopped listening haven't you?

DANTE: I am listening.

MASHUDU: I know I am a rambler, my mother said so. But this is so weird. Who knew we were all being listened to when we said "The Driving License Department was hell today so do yourself a favour and never go to the Randburg one." I didn't bring my ID do you think that matters?

DANTE: I cannot hope to ascertain what an ID, a passport or a driver's license is, without having us both being distracted from the task at hand. Let us be silent. The man before us is a soul you are fated to know. The disquieting moment before his confession will be worth our wait.

Minos takes out a few papers stapled together and then takes his glasses off the top of his head to quickly read them. He looks up with a numb expression. The dislodged soul shakes as he walks forward. Minos grows straighter and more formidable.

MINOS: Confess.

The bureaucrat places his hands together to mimic humble piety, he is stooped low.

BUREAUCRAT: (*squeaking*) There is a mistake; I am not supposed to be here.

MINOS: (*said with the annoyance of having had to repeat these lines a billion times*) Confess, for there has been no mistake.

BUREAUCRAT: You are a man of the bureaucracy, you know how we can find errors in the paperwork. Tippex is great my man. Do you have tippex? Because I think it is a good idea to just check for mistakes for me please.

MINOS: I do not make human mistakes. Confess.

BUREAUCRAT: I don't understand why I am here. I have been a simple man in my life. I found a job with the government. I followed the path with a wife who took care of me and kids who liked me enough to come for Sunday dinners. I simply grew old and died. Am I a sinner like the murderers all around me?

Minos growls and throws his tail on the table, with a grunt and heave of his shoulders. His inhumanness startles Mashudu.

MINOS: I do not have time to hear from you that you do not understand what brings you to Inferno. Confess.

BUREAUCRAT: (*desperately*) But I am not a sinner! Everyone says the apartheid government was villainous. But now everyone has been awful by saying I am the villain too. But how can I be a villain when I was just a lowly bureaucrat in one of the Population Registration Act offices? I did what I was told to do. I was ordered to classify people, which let me add, is no different from any other bureaucrat in any other country and so no different from you.

Minos slaps his tail on the table again. The bureaucrat in his desperation continues with conviction and forgets that his body feigned piety. He grows like a lizard, his spite makes him quick and frantic.

BUREAUCRAT: I was told that the most important thing about people was their skin colour. But this is no different from their date of birth, age and sex. The only thing is that for administrative purposes there needs to be a hierarchy of priority and the government wanted skin colour first. From one bureaucratic man to another— you must know that I was just part of the system, that I never really had a choice. I know there were cases where my classifications of people separated people from their families. But don't blame me, blame the mixing, the years of mixing! However, you have to understand that it was all to the service of the greater good of well done administrative work. (*spitefully*) You know that intimately don't you Minos? That is why I did rise up some ranks to suggest tiny improvements to the system. Not as high up as you though. I don't have an authoritative personality you see. But as I am sure you can understand this was just me being like any good employee wishing to do well at their job. It seems you must understand wanting to do well in your job too. But black was black and white was white. Everyone had to be separate, it was the only way people could be equal. This is no confession, it is an explanation. I am no sinner— I am only a gifted administrator. We are rare and should be cherished. Are you cherished?

Minos winds his tail smirking, as if he is relishing sending this sinner to eternity. His whole body circles with his tail, as if Minos is his own tornado. This is where the bureaucracy ends and justice begins.

BUREAUCRAT: Circle Eight... But I am not a sinner. I am like you Minos, I am you, I am you...

The bureaucrat is pulled by a powerful force. Sucked from the queue so his shouts of desperation grow dimmer and dimmer. Although his remorselessness seemed to still gather on the floor. Mashudu and Dante walk towards Minos. Mashudu is stifling her rage and presses her nails into her thumb. She realises the Dark Wood might have been easier in its stagnation. Minos grunts disapprovingly when he sees Dante and becomes hunched again over papers.

DANTE: I bring pleasant news Minos, you will not find our existence scrawled in your papers.

MINOS: Dante I see you have returned. Bored of the view from the mountain? Is one journey through the afterlife not enough?

DANTE: Ah Minos, some of us were always meant to be vagabonds. I do have to say I am overcome with a sense of elation to hear your teeth grinding once more.

MINOS: (*with a genuine bitter sadness*) Seems Purgatory has the monopoly of good dentists. I don't trust the ones in Inferno. Pity, my molars are really very painful. (*pauses*) I see you have brought another live one. What is with you poets? Ridiculous calling this pleasant news when now I have to fill in your exemption form.

DANTE: Inferno seems to be changing its face.

MINOS: Protocols are products of the times even in eternity.

Minos suddenly tilts his head towards Mashudu with curiosity.

MINOS: I see you other poet. Do you know you have arrived where the wretched dwell? Come here, so I can give you a warning. Watch how you enter. Inferno enjoys injecting its visitors with too much passion. Anger is not a very pretty emotion on young ladies.

Mashudu moves to speak but she sees Dante's hot, quick anger and steps back.

DANTE: Why this outburst? Do not obstruct her destined journey. Her path has been wished from the realm where whatever is desired demands to be realised. You have nothing more to say to her Minos.

Mashudu is surprised to see Dante's anger. She starts to truly understand that her journey is being ordered by a higher force. What she does not realise is that this was always the risk of becoming a poet. As Dante's anger subsides, melancholia pools at their feet. Mashudu's rage has turned into unnerving sadness. She is embraced by the significance of what she just saw. The past and present, magnetically interwoven had hurtled its way towards her. The afterlife wasn't some abstract space removed from her reality. The afterlife will be guiding her through her own reality. Her world wasn't distant, her world was here. She will not be able to hide from the truth of South Africa; it will be her reckoning. Yet, is this not the fate of poets? Is this not their burden? They reckon with our reality so that we have a path that allows us to have our own reckoning. The audience will have the privilege to walk with her. They will follow the path as it is immediately forged.

Mashudu creates a space for herself. Dante slowly enters it.

MASHUDU: I am sure what the sinner said does not have much meaning for you.

DANTE: The raving words of a sinner has the greatest meaning for those that know the sin intimately. I know that what he said has possessed that meaning for you.

MASHUDU: Too much meaning...I feel the stickiness of his remorselessness as if now I have to shoulder it, as if it has become my burden. My family lived in the same time of that man. Those left over still feel that time because of moments like this, the moments when the past comes too close. He was so happy determining our lives. He enjoyed classifying people in order to impose futures. My family is designated as black. We got pass books in 1950 in case our faces didn't prove it. Everyone inherits random genetics but yet we were the ones slapped with suffering in our hands. Proud of who we are but yet our backs still beaten. I feel my grandmother's wounds still. The sinner called himself a man of the system. I wonder how many of them Minos has seen. I wonder if all the cogs in the state's machine are here. Who would be missing and why? How many creatures of the system would I be able to find?

DANTE: You will not be able to meet all those from your world in Inferno. It is a place more limitless than our imaginings and time presses its hands against us, urging us to rush forward. The horror wants us to be still, perhaps we should be still. But we must go on.

MASHUDU: How can I know they are all here?

DANTE: Punishment is not judged as a collective over a group of people. Every person's sin is moulded on the contours of a whole life and so Minos receives the sinners one by one. Each receives their judgement in complete loneliness.

MASHUDU: I can't know they are all here can I?

Scene IV

Inferno Canto VII

The pilgrims bring the audience to a marsh that is fed by the river Styx. There is a pervasive haze and the stage is itself groggy and thick. The murkiness is its own kind of ruthlessness. The mud coats the pilgrim's feet as they breathe in an impenetrable fog. Mashudu and Dante feel the heaviness press down upon them as their limbs grow slower. They move with great difficulty through the marsh, it sometimes appears as if they are sinking. The pilgrims soon see bodies rise violently from the mud. The harsh weight pressed upon these bodies makes the viscousness of their movements more jarring. The audience is witnessing an endless fight. It is a cycle of ferocity in a peculiar way since it is not quickened. Rather the brutality of how fists hit jaws, knees meet ribs and limbs beat limbs is that one cannot lose sight of the damage caused. The fumes of the marsh crush the pilgrims who watch in disbelief. The can't stop gazing at the mud for in it is a weighted frenzy of cracked bones that will be broken for eternity. The sinners have no other purpose other than fighting each other, for they are forever bound to experience their own despotic rage. Teeth to flesh, fist to bone, the sinners bodies feed each other's abuse.

However, there is a strangeness to it. The heaviness gives way to unreality. The more the audience looks at the violence the more it looks like a choreographed dance. The desperation of the wrathful's movements would be rehearsed indefinitely. Each limb placed perfectly to ensure redemption would always be out of reach.

DANTE: "And I, who'd come to a halt to stand and gaze// Saw muddied people wallowing in the mire// All of them naked, all with looks of rage// And these, not only did they beat and beat// Each other with their fists, heads, breasts and feet// But tore each other piecemeal with their teeth." (109–114)

One of the wrathful is filled with the superiority of a man who knows how to use violence, embody violence and let his whole being be the talisman for his abusive power. His ego falls out of his grin as his body becomes lighter. He knows the dance so well, which allows him to step beyond it without the violence losing its timing. Though Mashudu and Dante know he would not miss out on continuing his punishment even with the pain. The pilgrims approach him cautiously.

WRATHFUL: Come nearer while my throat is free from the mud. You can only be lucky if you close to me, I am too sweet to be had at a distance. (*pauses*) Don't be afraid of the others. Or are you afraid of the dirt and the game? (*looks at Mashudu*) Does it matter if your clothes are torn? Does it matter if you receive a bruise? Scrape my body with your nails, I know you want to.

DANTE: We are not of those who delight in destruction.

The man completely ignores Dante and continues to stare at Mashudu.

WRATHFUL: Are you scared?

Mashudu gives an indignant look and rolls her eyes. He smiles so she can see that she stoked his anger. So she steps forward and looks him straight in the eye.

MASHUDU: Why would I be scared of you?

WRATHFUL: (*careful and calculated*) Good because I have to tell you I do not like frightened women. You pretty, maybe even pretty enough. But that doesn't change the hard facts that the women I like are women, not girls. I like my bed a little more dangerous. Could you give me that? Hmmm... I don't know. You look like a girl, seem like a girl. I am sure you are tight like a girl. Maybe when I was young I would have liked to lick you up. But I only want women now, I am set in my ways.

Mashudu tries not to look uncomfortable and so she remains silent. She doesn't want to give him any satisfaction yet can't help but feel scared that he would try touch her by reaching from the mud. So Mashudu leans a little back even though her feet are firmly in place. He cannot move from the mud but he displaces his head forwards so it looks as if he is about to bite.

WRATHFUL: Girl let me give you a lesson. (*gesturing to Dante*) Or does he already give you some? Maybe's he's already told you that when you get a woman she must know you are a man. There was one woman that I loved, one woman who was mine. I made her mine. You know, in all the right ways— nice things, protection, and those sweet words all women like to hear. I was a man for her, I did everything my father said I should. As a man, you must put down some rules. I lay down simple rules. Me coming first, that is just basic. Me being obeyed is just obvious. See, these rules are handed down to men because we are men. Adam was God's first creation and so my women owes me respect as she came from my own rib. That's what my dad told me. He told me that this truth is what makes a woman, a woman. Lay down the rules and a woman becomes your woman. My mother obeyed the rules and was happy because of them.

Mashudu can't stop herself from scoffing loudly. He looks at her with a passive aggressive charm. Dante looks ill at ease and panicked as he watches her.

MASHUDU: Happy? I wouldn't go that far.

WRATHFUL: Listen, baby girl. My woman, the woman who I made mine, couldn't follow my rules. Her body was good. She said she only gave it to me. Perhaps that was true, but that didn't change that when she broke the rules I got angry. So what do you do when you a man? You teach them what is right. So, I commanded her to be right, to be a woman. If she didn't listen and was being too stupid to learn, a slap or two was the only way. I loved her, but even what you love you got to set them straight when they are on the wrong path. Sweet words don't work. Would sweet words work on you and your hips?

DANTE: We can leave him alone to his anger now.

The man licks his lips and laughs. Dante tries to take Mashudu's hand so they can leave but yet Mashudu can't move. She knows the fate of the woman already but still needs to hear him say it. She needs to look her fear in the eye.

WRATHFUL: There was a problem though. My woman was not a real woman, she just became a girl. By the end she was just frightened in the corner. Why? I always wondered. Baby girl, you must know, I always liked her body less willing but I still needed that little fight back— she couldn't give that to me anymore. Instead of seeing that I was trying to right her wrongs she said I broke her. But come closer, let me tell you the truth, my father's truth. Real women don't break. Only girls break and there is nothing sexy about that, nothing about that you can give to me. It made me so angry, her limp body and that she couldn't look me in the eye. There was nothing that made her mine anymore. So listen here girl, you better be a woman or no man who is a real man will want you to be his. Like, I want to touch you but not really. Maybe when I was young I'd go at you hard but it would be no fun if you'd break.

Mashudu's eyes are shining. She is horrified but filled with a rage rushing from the core of her. She is overcome with the hatred of all her nightmares that can so easily turn real. She sees Dante's look of sympathy and turns back to him. She has nothing to say to this man despite her bitter fury.

WRATHFUL: See I knew you were a scared little girl. Want me to make you a woman?

Mashudu turns and runs towards him, her fist out ready to hit him. Her whole body is angled for an attack. The man doesn't even back away but stands proudly. Mashudu then suddenly pauses as she is about to hit him, gathers herself and stands just as proudly all to simply look at him. She just then smiles without breaking eye contact. He is taken aback as she looks at him with an expression that is sweet but patronising. She looks him up and down, raises her eyebrows and then laughs. She then gives him a thumbs up as if it say "Go Ahead, just try." The man is bothered by this and so his proud stance falters slightly. He is not used to condescension and suddenly realises his inability to do something about it. He is stuck in the mud. So he turns away to join the ferocity again.

As Mashudu turns around to face Dante her tears begin to stream down her face and her body caves in as she tries to breathe deeply. A sadness as violent as the wrathful beats its way through her.

DANTE: My words are lost. I do not think I can ease the burden locked around your heart. I do not know what is needed to allow you to breathe more easily again.

MASHUDU: I just need a moment before we continue. I don't know what I am supposed to feel.

Mashudu's whole body quietens and unravels. Dante is unsure of how much closer he can come to her in order to comfort her.

DANTE: I remember so clearly from my first journey a feeling so overpowering that I felt it surely would blind me.

MASHUDU: A desire to hurt?

DANTE: (*with a soft sympathy*) Very much so. It was a desire to hurt the souls of Inferno to an even greater extent than their punishment. Though what punishment that could have been was beyond what I could imagine. I could not conceive of a reality more painful than Inferno, but I wished that I could inflict the impossible on them. It was a feeling that shattered me.

MASHUDU: Insides like smashed glass. That is how my grandmother described anger. I just can't stop thinking about how I wanted to hurt him. That I hoped to be strong enough so that when I hit him he would feel it. It wouldn't have mattered that my fists could never be as powerful as Inferno. What would matter was that I was the one hurting him.

DANTE: You cannot forget that his punishment is for eternity. He will experience justice even beyond the time when time stops. There is justice in Inferno even if you are not the one inflicting it.

MASHUDU: I understand this. It is some comfort, only some. I cannot run away from my thoughts that if I hadn't stopped myself (*pauses*), if I had given into the screaming voice inside of me that wanted revenge.... (*with a whisper*) I would be just like him. I would deserve to be skinless in the mud.

DANTE: He is a mirror without a reflection of the truth of his monstrous form. Why do you proclaim with no hesitancy or questioning, that you would be a copy of his barren remorselessness? Anger may possess you, but how can you think your being could hold such ruthlessness?

Dante can recognise that Mashudu is in pain but is searching for the depth of it. He understands he is dislocated from her world and so is lost in terms of what to do. How does he guide what he doesn't know? The horror of the man affected him too but yet he couldn't grasp why this woman's fate felt so close to her. Slowly he understood that Mashudu was in mourning for the woman. Her rage at both the man and herself was her helplessness. Mashudu's anger was the fury of a kind of grief.

DANTE: You can mourn for her. I can see your unrelenting grief.

MASHUDU: She must have felt so trapped. She must have felt so alone. I hope she had some chance yet I know this didn't happen. A woman dying doesn't mean much to a man like that.

DANTE: If she did not survive his hand, know that she will also be treated by justice.

MASHUDU: I don't understand.

DANTE: Justice is more than retribution, what is divine is also about deliverance.

MASHUDU: Is she safe?

DANTE: She is with God.

MASHUDU: Dante, the divine then came too late. Do not tell me that the divine didn't come too late.

Mashudu sits down to cry while Dante stands behind her. His body dejected by not knowing what to do.

VIRGIL: Mashudu went to therapy for this what all modern poets do. Although she could obviously not tell her therapist the real way she met this man. As a poet she knows she cannot risk it because those of the profession are already considered mad, too mad, a mad with no chance of being saved. The therapist suggested that she write about it. "Writing is soothing" the therapist said. The first poem Mashudu wrote was filled with swear words and curses against the man, God and the world. This is not worth repeating to an audience who might have heavenly soaked ears. Her mother read it and said that it just seemed like she didn't know how to use a thesaurus. Her father said her anger was not innovative. So one night Mashudu took it seriously and wrote a poem in rebellion against all that this man was. It is called Frightened Woman, Scared Little Girl. I will read the last verse for you.

"I have waltzed down to the riverbank quite alone// Singing and choosing flowers// With the knowledge that what needs to be defeated// Is never the fragility that true divine grace enters through// I have had the flowers turn to me// While finding myself understanding what I am singing// I, the frightened woman, the scared little girl// Will be divine// Because I stopped before I raised my fist."

Scene V

Inferno Canto XII

The stage is a vivid pulsating red, as if we are thrust into the middle of a heart that beats wrongly. The red tastes of asphyxiation as we are submerged. We hear sounds of water popping as the red froths over at the edges of the stage. The pilgrims appear like wounds. Standing on the red banks, Mashudu and Dante see a river of blood the colour of burst arteries. They begin to walk carefully with their heads peering over the river and their bodies tied to the shore. It is the Phlegathon, the river belonging to the memories of the brutal. It is the river that loves its sacrificial victims to be burnt but never lets them drown. The Phlegathon enjoys erupting so flesh can disintegrate. Its water yearns for skin to melt off bones. The whole of Inferno has been lost in shadows but here the shadows radiate red.

DANTE: "We went beside the boiling crimson river// I heard the high-pitched shrieks of those being boiled.// I saw some there up to their eyebrows under//…Then I saw people keeping their heads raised// And even their whole chests, above the river//" (100–103…121–122)

MASHUDU: Who are they Dante?

DANTE: "…They are tyrants// Who liked to soak their hands in blood and plunder// They pay for pitiless brutality." (104–106)

A policeman rises out of the river. His apartheid police uniform is pocketed with burnt holes that show how his skin is rippled with red blisters and cracking open. The policeman is almost as red as the river, his skin is raw and exposed. His flesh is almost too alive. He is now a man without a shell. Behind the policeman are red figures like ghosts. It is as if an army has emerged from the river. Yet, only this man has the burden of a body. He is the vessel that allows a chorus of voices to spill out like uncooked meat. The chorus can only be described as a the monotonous drawl of a drill.

The voices are simply forgeries of each other. They are apparitions like festering sores and they shimmer around the lone policeman.

POLICEMAN I: We as the police of old South Africa remember. We remember how the coldness of our heated guns shot into unarmed people. Our hands had burns that felt like ice while our dead victims were not as cold. So we still shot for there were not enough victims and we didn't need to heal when our hands were numb. We as the police of old South Africa remember. We remember the rips of the bullets and how they sang before they collided with bone. We remember the screams but because they were not our screams they were too cold to feel. But now we burn in blood. Whether it is our victim's blood or our own it matters little. We are finally screaming.

There is still a chorus but now there are a few voices repeating "we remember and so we burn"

POLICEMAN I: (*raises his hands to look at them*) This is the screaming we care about. This is the screaming that counts. Our skins are scorched. We feel the heat of the gun only now. We remember 1960 in Sharpeville and 1976 in Soweto and feel the pain of our blistered hands. In Soweto they were only children yet we heated the sky. Although we must not let you forget that we followed corpse-cold orders. That is what we say when our blood spits fire. Guilt was there for some but not for all. Some felt their hands burn before they died, they had death on their minds. (*snaps hands down in rage*) Those who feel guilt do not understand that the wrongness doesn't lie with us but those who gave the orders. We were soldiers of justice not the inventors of it. We were just a police force that was a military gone to war. We shot the gun and now our hearts have turned to sand. But who ordered the gun? Who gave our bodies to the blaze? We know of the destruction and devastation we caused. But we will not repent. There is too much blood to think of anything other than our screams. We remember and so we burn.

Mashudu and Dante are silent as the voices that are chanting are folded into the redness. The chorus of the past cannot be replicated when the present comes to rise from the river. The pilgrim's see one lone policeman of the new South Africa come out of the blood but with no red ghosts behind him. The past accumulates the dead like trophies so that the choir of the damned can stretch beyond the stage. It is the present that does not have enough of the dead. Twenty-eight years is enough time for the new South Africa to be known to Inferno. But how known will the new South Africa be in the next twenty-eight years? Will the new South Africa be intimate with damnation? It is the future that is always the question.

POLICEMAN II: (*spoken restlessly*) I was part of the police of the new South Africa and I remember. I remember the blood, the bullets, and the miners. I remember that I loved the heat of the gun because it was my own. It mattered little that they were protesting. What mattered was the chaos. I saw them as destructive fires. They were going to burn it all down, including me. I said my gun was scorching for a better South Africa. I said they provoked us, I told them all that they led us to open fire. Maybe that is still true. But up until the moment my heart gave in I felt no guilt. I did not have nightmares of the barbed wire and the blood dropped in the dust. I didn't wake up sweating after remembering how I heated the sky. I thought I was right, no one could tell me other truths. So now I am waiting for my friends to join me. I'll wait though their hearts were not as weak as mine. I am waiting for us to blister together, in blood thicker than the blood we spilt. But I might always be lonely. The new South Africa could rob me of merciless friends. I should have let South Africa burn for I am screaming more than the miners ever did, but unlike me, they weren't screaming alone.

Dante turns away from the policemen. It is only Mashudu who pauses with a questioning expression.

Scene VI

Inferno Canto XXXII

Inferno has turned into ice. The shadows echo as their reflections ripple against the frozen landscape. As the pilgrims walk across the icy plane their shoes are pierced as if by glass, creating a shock that runs through their bodies. The cold turns the air into blades so Mashudu and Dante have to constantly pause to try breathe in properly, although their lungs are shredded like paper. The land cracks and hisses under their weight leaving them perilously off centre. Mashudu then attempts to scream but her voice is rendered silent, so her body has to scream for her. The cold cannot stop the shock of seeing the bodies frozen painfully into inhumane patterns of limbs. The sinner's bodies mutilated like dolls ripped apart at the joints. Their limbs are contorted mercilessly. Yet nothing could be as sickening as the grotesque and swollen heads. Their contorted facial expressions map a kind of annihilation. Some of them even rise just above the ice, which makes Mashudu realise how many faces she must have crushed. Those blue tinged heads with their eyes that blink unevenly, were definitely alive though they were trapped. They were unable to even shiver. And so the pilgrims shivered for them as eerie silence continues to swirl through the space. The Inferno of heat and fire was filled with the unrested noise of damnation. Now the silence, like an avalanche that has come to rest, holds the cold in place. The ice a prison for the voices of those who should not speak. They had too great a voice in life and so need to be silenced in Inferno. Their pain is their new incapacitated helplessness. Therefore, let it be noted, how arrogant a voice had to be to believe he was entitled to reclaim his right to speak.

JAN: (*a haughty anger, with a body still frozen and rigid*) You over there, coloured girl, and you, who is obviously her master. Come here, you kicked my face!

Mashudu stops and whispers to Dante.

MASHUDU: I know it is Jan van Riebeeck and because I know who he is I have decided to ignore him.

JAN: (*his head is snakelike as it rises from the ice*) You are her master, why are you not disciplining her? A coloured girl should not act out to any man like this. Let alone a man of my stature.

Dante looks at Mashudu with sympathy in his eyes. She knows that he is about to say that he is one of the souls in her journey she has to engage with. How else could she reckon with the reality of South Africa, without knowing the man who turned the land's history upside down?

MASHUDU: I know, I know... those in Paradise have commanded it. You don't need to tell me. Well, let us just get on with it, since I'd rather be stuck to a chair and forced to hear nails scrape against a chalkboard for a week. (*shouting at Jan van Riebeeck*) I may recognise your face but that doesn't mean I owe anything to you.

Jan van Riebeeck gestures to Dante with his head, to discipline Mashudu.

DANTE: I believe clarity is needed in this situation. I serve her. I am not her master, I am her servant on her mission commanded by the divine. She is here by God's grace.

JAN: (*his body starts slithering up from the ice*) Impossible.

DANTE: (*asking Mashudu*) Who is this man with such a malformed face? Why is he imprisoned in the ice?

Mashudu gives Dante a look as if to say "Have we not done enough? Do we have to start with his one please?" But Jan van Riebeeck interrupts before she can even begin. His body becomes wormlike as it comes up from the cracks in the ice. Jan van Riebeeck's eyes narrow as he smiles; he knows she won't give him glory.

JAN: Unfortunately, it does not seem that you will grant me the curtesy I am owed by introducing me to your master. So, I am going to introduce myself. (*dramatically and flamboyantly*) My name is Jan van Riebeeck of the Dutch East India Company. I was the commander of the Dutch settlement in the Cape of Good Hope. I was the father of Cape Town. What word describes my nature? How can I embody my own existence? The word is "genius." I was a genius that birthed South Africa. It was my hands that lay the foundation for a land to enter into history for the first time. Everyone must know how close the chance was for history to never come to South Africa. Fortunately, to be a genius is to be a rebel. Let me admit that even though I was the origins of South Africa, I was initially told not to colonise the Cape. I was told to build a fort and build a fort only. Yet it is a genius that has the imagination for possibility. I was always destined to be glorious.

MASHUDU: Why am I not surprised that he has this rehearsed?

Jan van Riebeeck ignores her. He transforms his body again now into the strong willed frame of a man with ego. He shoulders look like a wide coat-hanger.

JAN: There was so much land that belonged to no one. It was a land of emptiness although a fertile land. All it needed was a great hand to give it a mission. The land could serve but it needed to be used properly. It needed to be used the Dutch way. A genius never begs, a genius persuades and so I showed the company the brilliant worth of settlement. The land was just sitting there but our farmers could dominate it to our will. I am sure your history books must have already told you this, because I am a man of history. I changed the fate of the land when my genius brought into existence the colony. I had the gifts, the mind, the power, so I had a duty to have something done with the untouched before me. Or should I say—the potential. Everyone thought I was glorious. Do you not think so coloured girl?

MASHUDU: (*she tenses up*) I think you seem to pick and choose your memories. Do you not remember the people you found when you arrived? Do you not remember the people who really belonged to the land? It was not empty, us black people had already put our souls into the soil.

JAN: They were not very rememberable if I am to be honest. Why would I remember them?

MASHUDU: Do you not remember that you drove them from their lands? Do you not remember who you are?

JAN: I know exactly who I am. I am Jan van Riebeeck of the...

Mashudu cuts him off as he is about to begin his speech again. Her head turns to emphasise her accusation.

MASHUDU: And the land you stole?

JAN: What? You mean I stole from those black migrating pastoralists? Those who moved their cattle to different grazing lands? Those who believed the land was alive? They were idiotic nomads. They didn't know what it truly meant to own the land. (*his chest puffs out, he seems snakelike again*) You can only know the land, use the land if you possess the land.

MASHUDU: I see, domination is your only language even with plants.

JAN: They knew we knew better and that is why their fight for the land was so pathetic. That is why they eventually would need our God.

MASHUDU: I realise it is too much to ask a man like you to think let alone reflect. My mistake.

JAN: What is there to reflect on if I have been wrongly accused? I deserve glory because I am glorious. If I was alive I would not have to suffer this humiliation.

Mashudu cannot stop this conversation although it is infuriating her. We could say that it is because she wants to truly know if her imaginings of Jan van Riebeeck were hyperbolic in terms of his arrogant racism. She saw it for what it was—delusions. Nevertheless, as she continued she was shocked at how deep those delusions would go. He was out touch of reality in general not just a moral reality. What was painful for Mashudu to realise was that these delusions didn't just belong to Jan van Riebeeck but to many. These delusions had roots in a company, a country and a continent. Therefore even though these beliefs are irrational with no truth behind them, the heartbreak and the fury comes in that these delusions of racist, colonial grandeur would destroy the land and the people that put their souls in the soil, limb from limb.

MASHUDU: Perhaps shame could be a good emotion for you.

JAN: (*appalled*) Shame? Me? I have never felt shame in my life.

MASHUDU: Let us be reasonable. It seems the rational response is to feel shame when you are trapped in the circle dedicated to the betrayers of their country.

JAN: (*mocking*) Let us be reasonable. (*with a shade of anger*) I am reasonable. I would never betray my country or my company. Even my letter for settlement was following due procedure.

DANTE: (*calm but accusatory*) I doubt the truth lies comfortably on your lips. This does not worry us for divine justice always draws out honesty from the mouth of a sinner. What did justice find when it moved into the heart of you? What confession was forced from your tongue in front of Minos, to seal your fate?

JAN: What I said could not have been true. I jabbered like something so uncivilised.

MASHUDU: Looks like your confession will be the closest thing you've come to civilisation.

JAN: I cannot speak with this kind of hostility I am not one to be defamed.

Jan van Riebeeck now has an audience and even though he has claimed defamation, he is secretly so happy to perform his role as "Jan van Riebeeck." It was as if his ego and self were both one and they were too large to only be encapsulated in a single performance. There was a flamboyance, a desire to play the role of the powerful genius, the role of the real man and master of fate. The shifts in his body from rigid to snaking and then to egotistical shoulders, showed that he would transform himself in all possible ways just to be seen and known. All he desired was to be noticed because he feared insignificance. And yet, among all the putrid heads, he couldn't claim his power was unique. There are many ways to describe Jan van Riebeeck— brutal, violent, racist, a rapist, cruel—all of them rooted in a desire for power. Jan van Riebeeck doesn't have much power stuck in the ice as his puppet body is cruelly played with by the cold. His only grasp of power is now to dominate his own identity as it has not been safe in the hands of history. Jan van Riebeeck doesn't know how he became the villain.

JAN: (*spitefully*) My condemnation was that my betrayal was deeper than turning one's back on one's country for I betrayed the land. I should have honoured the land I stepped onto but I did not. I dishonoured the souls buried in the soil. I was compelled to declare my violent possessiveness. I felt the involuntary pressure to admit that the settlement was an act of power that poisoned the ground despite our European prosperity. (*pauses*) Can you not hear how empty this condemnation is?

MASHUDU: Doesn't seem so empty to me.

JAN: You do not understand the world or men. This is an injustice that has been tyrannically forced out of me. I was under duress! I cry defamation! I honoured the land by giving the land purpose and even more importantly, a Dutch East India Company purpose, a Dutch purpose, a European purpose.

MASHUDU: A white purpose.

JAN: I gave the land its rightful life under rightful command. Yet I am also condemned for more than my own actions of genius and supreme creation. I am held hostage by the history that came after it.

DANTE: Our fate is always determined by the consequences that belong to us.

JAN: I do not believe that the history that is mine is worth my pain. My people made the land their own with their own tongue. They didn't dishonour the land as there was no other land that could be theirs. I made it theirs. If I shall be punished let my people know I am being punished for giving them their whole world.

MASHUDU: Your great mission came at a price.

JAN: (*scoffs*) Yes I know the British are included in all this. Did you know I suffer their burden as well? And they certainly do not recognise my gloriousness.

MASHUDU: You are exactly as I expected. Thank you, you have given me confidence in my own judgement.

JAN: Am I to be condemned for being a man of my times? Am I to be villainised for being exactly what my era demanded of me?

MASHUDU: History is turning on you.

JAN: Remember, when you throw your unjustified blame on me that you should not forget the British. I am sure the British would have colonised anyway. They would not have done it as brilliantly as me, they never had the Dutch brilliancy. But the whole world was dying for Africa. The land was empty, there was always going to be a scramble.

MASHUDU: I never thought geniuses enjoyed following the crowd.

JAN: I was the creator, I was the father of South Africa. I birthed Cape Town. Cecil Rhodes, Lord Milner, the British came after me! They are also trapped somewhere here. Go find them, I am tired of you. Kick their heads in too, it seems like you get a sadistic rush from torturing the vulnerable. (*turns to Dante*) Rein her in my dear man! I have never liked those smart coloured girls. They are too snappy, they are too free.

MASHUDU: The words from men with no glory don't hold much weight do they?

Jan van Riebeeck looks visibly upset by Mashudu's presence. He in fact looks like he is about to cry with the expression of a child on the verge of a tantrum. He snakes his way back into the ice

MASHUDU: Dante, we have moved through Inferno and I do not see any remorse. No one feels any guilt. Please tell me, how can these punishments be real if they do not feel any guilt? How can Jan van Riebeeck be said to feel justice if he still believes in his own greatness?

DANTE: I believe he is still punished. Do you not?

MASHUDU: It seems he is only punished physically. It looks uncomfortable but is it punishment? He can certainly slither out the ice.

DANTE: I believe there is tremendous punishment when one feels that they are owed or deserve glory but they do not receive anything but shame and torture. I believe that the man was performing his old self, one last chance to be what he used to be.

MASHUDU: But he has no remorse.

DANTE: Remorse is a difficult truth. Some men can alter the fate of their minds in an instant when they understand how they have been misguided. Some men they need time to unfold before they can recognise and be remorseful. The last kind of men cannot alter their minds at all. I am afraid he is the last-mentioned and that is why he is here.

MASHUDU: Isn't that the easier path?

DANTE: I do not think so. His punishment is worsened by his lack of remorse. This is because he cannot change. He can only wither away with the pain of being insignificant or at the very least known to be an imposter to greatness, when greatness is all that he has ever wanted.

MASHUDU: I want him to be remorseful even if the punishment is fair. I want him to understand what he did.

DANTE: Do you want him to be saved? His great sin is his ignorance of the magnitude of his wrong-doing. When he understands the truth of his actions he can repent, ask for forgiveness. Remorse is the beginning of being saved.

Mashudu brings her fingers to her temples and breathes in deeply.

MASHUDU: So the options are, him having the chance of being saved or there being no acknowledgement of the damage he caused? Is that justice? Is that fair? The damage he did was deliberate. He is not completely ignorant.

DANTE: Knowing how to hurt is very different to knowing why it is wrong.

MASHUDU: I don't understand Inferno, do I?

Scene VII

Inferno Canto XXXIV

The possibility of redemption had been captured by Inferno and held hostage with no ransom. Now, as we find ourselves within the last circle of hell, redemption has finally been killed. It is a massacre of goodness. Nothing can escape the desolation. The barrenness hides the truth that there is nothing about this world other than suffering. Suffering is the ground and the glass air. Suffering is the silence as well as the heaves and sobs of the ice. Suffering is the gales that suddenly break the landscape. A doomed sorrow sat with the pilgrims as well as the fury of a realm created for the ultimate form of divine justice. What do you do with a world that abandoned even the dignity of punishment for something else entirely? Only what is as wrong as the Devil can create a place so unnatural. Suffering had the purpose of stripping meaning to its bones to snap them. Suffering scattered what was real to the wind for it to never return.

Mashudu is filled with the impenetrability of a sorrow that she couldn't break apart with her bare hands even if she wanted to. Her worry was that she was losing the meaning of being human. The pain had buried itself so deep under her skin that she was frightened she would give up her humanity just to take the pain away.

MASHUDU: I want to stop looking. Will this ever leave me?

DANTE: You will never escape this vision for I have never escaped it. Your memories will become revenants.

The image of the Devil comes into view for the audience. The Devil is a giant although we only see his chest and face rise from the ice that has locked him in. The Devil has three faces that are joined together at the neck. Under each face there are two monstrous wings, which are not feathered but are made from skin. When these wings are beaten, blasts of wind reverberate against the edges of the circle of hell and shake the circle's epicentre. The six eyes of the Devil are filled with tears that come to drip down his cheeks to mix with his bloody saliva. Every mouth is filled with multiple sets of teeth, which allow the Devil to grind up a sinner. The sinner in front's spine was in sight.

The pilgrims stand completely still, side by side with their shoulders touching. It is not the stillness of being calm, instead their breath is shallow. The pilgrims bodies are in shock and their voices are being attacked by panic. They then begin to speak in a disjointed union. It is Dante's extension of friendship for Mashudu cannot describe properly what she is witnessing because her shock is so raw. Dante thought he would be able to face the horror. Since he witnessed it before, he prayed he would be stronger. Instead, the anguish feels more acute as he is confronting both this moment and the moment of his past. Dante uses his poetry to give Mashudu language in the face of the nightmare.

MASHUDU: (*touching her cheeks*) Those six eyes... tears, so many tears.

DANTE: "With six eyes he was weeping, down three chins// The tears were dripping, mixed with bloody slaver." (53)

MASHUDU: (*touching her lips*) Too many teeth, those mouths that claw... the bodies torn, skin like ribbons.

DANTE: "In every mouth, as with a rake or comb// The teeth were screaming, grinding up a sinner" (54-55)

MASHUDU: (*grabs Dante's hand and flinches*) Three sinners...I see so much pain... sinners. Pain, unimaginable yet I can feel it... I can't look but I know I must.

DANTE: "There were three simultaneously in pain// And yet to him in front being so gnawn// Seemed nothing to the clawing: very often// The sinner's back was bared down to the bone." (56-60)

MASHUDU: I can't look but I know I must.

They pause for a moment. They are braver in the face of the horror that they have named together. Their descriptions did not bring calmness but nevertheless it did renew their strength. Mashudu finally feels she can step away from Dante's frame. She now knows what she is witnessing and so knows her own fear.

MASHUDU: I want to know that the pain in front of me has a purpose.

DANTE: This means that you are ready to know the sinners. "The emperor of the empire of despair" holds in his mouth the monsters of your world as he did mine (28). Look closely at their faces to know the reason for their fates. Just as I have done before. You know them and so you must tell me who they are for I do not know the truth of your reality. Who haunts you?

Mashudu leans forward and stares. As a slow recognition comes upon her she steps back as if she is scared they are contagious.

MASHUDU: Haunting, they are a haunting. I will name them not for their sake but for mine. They have no more power being cut clean by the Devil. They will never be free. Hendrik Verwoerd, John Vorster, P.W Botha I see how you have all been violated and left without dignity. I cannot help but believe this is what justice looks like.

DANTE: The cruelty of justice has always been a rational insanity.

MASHUDU: These three sinners, Dante, have imaginations worse than the Devil and so they deserve to be returned to the Devil to be tortured. It feels good to know that death never let them escape.

DANTE: Judgement is the only certainty in the afterlife. This is for every man whether human or monster. Now, tell me the truth that I do not know.

MASHUDU: I can't explain the hatred of these men. I don't know how they became one with it. I am still wondering how they could create a regime like they did. I don't know how someone could envision apartheid and summon it into reality.

They had so much hatred but they were too cruel to be mad. I see there is justice and I have to say, Dante I am relieved. But there is still something bothering me.

DANTE: What can it be? The ultimate form of justice has been realised.

MASHUDU: I know justice has been acted out, I see Verwoerd's spine. Still this doesn't change what they have left behind. Their actions were of a magnitude so great that the consequences have sent shockwaves into the present. We are still trying to escape from their claws. It gives me peace that they will never escape from the devil. But Dante... but... but....

DANTE: What is missing for you?

Mashudu turns directly to the audience, her body holds a melancholic stillness. Mashudu is not only addressing Dante but is talking to her family, her friends, the strangers of the land she belongs to. She is considering her questions as not just belonging to her.

MASHUDU: Dante the only thing on my mind is the question of whether I could truly describe the pain and terror of apartheid to you? How do I describe the truth? I am all out of language. Sometimes what has happened is indescribable. Sometimes truths are beyond words. I can tell you the facts but they cannot tell you the reality.

DANTE: "There is no tongue in which it could be told" (24). I too have not known how to describe cruelty.

MASHUDU: It is unthinkable when I try to say it out loud. I am born into a democracy but democracies have pasts. We are hurting. How can we not be in pain when we carry so many memories? What do I do with the memories that I have inherited? What do we all do with the consequences that are as deep as the memories? And I as a black woman carry so much of that burden. I carry so much of that weight. (*pauses*) Some people believe there should just be forgetfulness. They believe in deliberately losing our memories. It is a prayer for collective amnesia as they say it is the only way to reconciliation. Is this the only way to step forward into the future? Where it is not enough to forgive, one needs to forget?

DANTE: (*walking closer to stand behind her, he puts a hand on her shoulder*) Is it right to lose one's memory? Does it honour those that have suffered?

MASHUDU: I don't know. Maybe those who come from the past are better off if we forget about them. Maybe they will be at peace without our memories disturbing them.

DANTE: Do you truly believe this? Are you being true? When will you begin to will yourself to forget?

MASHUDU: (*rises higher*) No...I won't let myself forget. I want to remember, I need to remember.

DANTE: To remember the past is to come to know and understand our present complications. It has always been so.

MASHUDU: (*quietly and desperately while looking at her hands*) Dante I wish I had more answers. I wish language was closer to me. Instead my hands are filled with memories but I am empty of words. My head hurts from the memories of my parents, my grandparents, my aunts and uncles. Where do I put their grief down? Where do I put my own grief down?

DANTE: Your burden is that the language that reckons with this past is for you to create.

Mashudu walks away and crouches down, knees on chest in order to contain her emotion. The weight of her reckoning was a burden she felt she couldn't bear. Dante may be her guide but he cannot truly understand the pain that pressed into her shoulders. She wondered if she was being clawed like Verwoerd, but for her it would be from the inside. She quickly let go of the thought. Her pain was not punishment, that is an easier pain in many ways. Her pain was complicated, messy, beyond her comprehension yet she could feel it so vividly. It was a pain that needed language but was there any language for such devastation? She slowly began to understand what Dante meant that she would have to create the language herself. She would have to use language as a weapon to remember the past and bring justice. She would have to use language to never let the truth go.

Dante comes to Mashudu and draws her up. She is confused as he leads her to the edge of the wasteland and tilts her chin up as he points up to the sky. She looks up and her eyes open wider. Mashudu gasps to see a sky that holds the tapestry of a million stars. Light falls out of the fractures in the atmosphere.

DANTE: Look up. Do you not see how we have "emerged to look once more upon the stars." Do you see the glory of the heavenly spheres? (139)

MASHUDU: We have arrived somewhere. Dante where are we?

DANTE: It is time to tell me the story of the beautiful ways of being that cannot be forgotten. Tell me what you will one day write.

MASHUDU: There is beauty. I do know this.

DANTE: The beauty must be known. Inferno demands an answer.

MASHUDU: (*suddenly her body looks exhausted*) I am so tired Dante. Can I tell you after I have slept?

DANTE: We will sleep on the beach. Please answer me first. If there is beauty and if that beauty can be known, does this mean there is hope?

MASHUDU: (*with a bittersweetness*) Yes there is hope. There has always been hope.

Part Two: Purgatory

Scene VIII

Purgatory Canto I

A yellow light with a loose touch runs through the theatre making it soft and warm. Just the light itself feels like a deliverance even though Paradise is still a whole world away. The decaying hands of Inferno's shadows have let the pilgrims go. There is a sense of possibility again. The light then opens itself to the scene of a beach with crisp and golden sand. The sand cradles the bodies of the pilgrims. Mashudu's mind gives into the warmth of her relief and she lets the gentle sand fall from her fingers in hourglass patterns. She feels time but ignores it. The beach is its own kind of elsewhere, it is a realm that could only belong to the in-between. The pilgrims have been received by what is beyond the fire and ice and so can finally feel that their wounds are beginning to be stitched closed. The despair is losing its power and we can see it in how their bodies finally find an ease in their breathing. However, it is not a resurrection, they have not been shrouded in grace. Redemption has not been conferred, it could never come so easily. Rather, it is a temporary moment of sanctuary. It is an ephemeral heart beat that allows divine justice to rest as well. This can only be fleeting for the new Cato is sure to arrive. The beginning has been summoned again and now feels the joy of the wide expanse of blue sky and the tender light trailing down from the heavens.

Behind the beach, reaching up like a promise, is the Mountain of Purgatory. It is too tall to even fit in the sky. The Mountain lifts itself up towards the being that created it as the sunlight hits its skin so its cracks burn gold. Its beauty is an invitation although it does not hide the challenge it offers like a gift. The steepness of the climb to come is its own sense of vertigo.

Mashudu takes out a notebook from her pocket and begins to write. She occasionally looks up with a perplexed imprint on her face but then it melts into an expression of gentle authority. Dante looks at her and smiles. Virgil then saunters across the stage with his sunglasses and beach shorts. He flamboyantly holds a coke with a straw. His hips are loose and his gaze holds a smirk.

VIRGIL: (*becoming grander with each sentence*) Now, good audience, we find our two pilgrims washed ashore on the island of Mount Purgatory. Pity it is the afterlife and pity the Greeks are in **Limbo**. See this would be such a good place for a party. **Limbo** is so dark. Our shadowed valley and sad abyss is not the worst neighbourhood Inferno has to offer I will admit. But, we all know how good the day drunk vibe is. I know what you're thinking— the man is in **limbo**, dark or not that must be a party everyday. Yes, we have Heraclitus and he smokes only the good weed. And Socrates? Well, don't need to say much about that. You know Aristotle? He gets wine drunk like a suburban queen. But, I say with pain in my heart, that the Romans are just disappointing. Cicero is just messy and Ovid is very petty when high. I may be a good pagan soul who yearns for God but I still know how to have a good time, as pagans do. But a beach party would have been so nice. See I am glad to have you guys. Sometimes you need the thrill of a new crowd: test the waters of your humour, try a new cocktail mix. Thank you dear audience! I am delivered from boredom and Aurelius's speeches!

There is a whisper in the wings and Virgil quickly runs to the play technician. It looks as if he is being reprimanded with fingers being pointed and Virgil rolling his eyes. Yet he comes back grinning like a child, with a quickness to his step.

VIRGIL: Gosh, so rude... Apparently I am taking over the story. Let me start again. We find our pilgrims washed ashore on the island of Mount Purgatory. Look at Dante, what a poet. Only a poet can have that romantic lethargy. Look at them both, the languor of the poets, the ennui of the poets. Their drowsiness makes their daydreams so slow you can touch them. Don't expect the poets to be all action like those heroes in epic poems. Don't expect poets to be as impulsive as every superhero in those movies with the same plot repeated and action scenes (it is amazing, they are all so similar in how effectively they induce boredom). They will act, instead, with the care of language. They will pause to let the world in to be able to write it more vividly, to be able to write it more truthfully. I call it the technique of poetic pensiveness. It is very important as it heralds to the Muses that the poets are ready for what comes next because they have taken the time to understand what came before. Can you see Mashudu writing? Can you see masterpieces unravelling at the bottom of mountains like all masterpieces should?

Mashudu reads over what she has written and then puts her notebook away. As if it was the act of freeing her mind in the words that electrified her with energy. She jumps up like a bolt of lightning in the wrong direction and grabs Dante's hand to pull him up from the sand. Their exhaustion has escaped from their limbs and so they can now echo each other in their relief. But Dante is still hesitant as he knows intimately the challenge of the Mountain. He is a creature of Purgatory after all. But Dante will not spoil her happiness, she will know soon enough. A burden lifted even when lifted fleetingly is a priceless thing to witness.

MASHUDU: (*laughing*) My mind is setting sail, Dante.

DANTE: Tell me, how does it feel to set sail on God-favoured waters? How does it feel to leave the sea of cruelty behind?

MASHUDU: (*breathing deeply*) It feels good. It just feels so good.

DANTE: "And now I sing in rhyme that second reign// There where the human spirit is made worthy// To soar to Heaven, being purged of sin." (4-6)

MASHUDU: Dante do you dance?

Dante shakes his head, crosses his arms and tries to back away. Mashudu simply follows laughing.

DANTE: I am a man of exile, I do not dance.

MASHUDU: But how do I invoke the Muses without dancing? You cannot let me dance alone on this beach.

DANTE: I am more than 700 years old. I am too old to dance.

MASHUDU: Almost all that time you have been dead which means it doesn't count.

Mashudu holds Dante's hand and awkwardly tries to teach him how to waltz. She then stops and lets go of Dante. She turns to face the mountain, opens her arms and tilts her head towards the light. She shouts as loud as she can so the heavens can shake and the Muses can hear her.

MASHUDU: "And here, Calliope come to my aid // And lend my utterance a more lofty tone." (9-10)

Dante recognises his own poetry and smiles. He then begins to shout the lines with Mashudu. He feels the gold warmth of his care for her that has steadily grown through their journey. The divine did not just find another poet for him to guide, they found him a friend.

MASHUDU & DANTE: "Here raise my inspiration from the dead// O sacred Muses, since I am all yours," (7-8)

Mashudu and Dante suddenly pause and turn their heads to watch the solitary figure that has appeared on the beach. An ancient nobility surrounds him as he walks for he has now taken the role of the guardian of Purgatory. It is only men that know the truth about justice and the responsibility of freedom that have followed the footsteps of Cato. It is a role of great sacrifice as one must guide souls towards their ascension and not climb the mountain oneself. Mashudu slowly recognises the figure cloaked in both purpose, discipline and duty, as John Dube. Instantly, Mashudu becomes serious. John Dube is a man that commands respect.

DUBE: Pilgrims, we finally meet. I now am the one who holds Cato's burden. Tell me all.

DANTE: I have been summoned to guide this woman through the realms of the afterlife. This duty was bestowed upon me by virtuous souls that you kindly share a history with Mr John Dube. We have come from the Infernal darkness but are in no way damned. I can speak of the legitimacy of her journey.

John Dube looks past Dante and straight to Mashudu. She cannot escape his gaze, nor does she want to. She understands that to be apprehended is to begin to be known and she hopes to be known by John Dube as someone who is good. All she wanted was insight and guidance on the question of why she was chosen to travel through the afterlife. She didn't mind if the answer was difficult or easy, complicated or simple, she was just tired of the unknown and the doubt.

DUBE: I have known about your journey, as I was told by the souls in Paradise. The moment now calls for me to enact my role. Dante, I recognise you for I too am a poet. However, as you must acknowledge, a poet's words need to come from a poet's mouth. I would like to hear from this woman before me. Tell me about your travels.

Mashudu's keeps her head down with her eyes looking up fleetingly. She did not respect a soul in Inferno and so she had all the confidence in the world to claim her own authority. But John Dube was different—her family revered him and so suddenly she felt so uncertain under the microscope of his watchfulness.

MASHUDU: Baba John, it is an honour to be in your presence. So much of my own freedom is owed to you and I am grateful. I don't know what to say of my own journey. It hardly feels as if I have lived it. I don't think I can tell you exactly what it means. I want to blame it on me being young, but, I don't know if you would accept my answer. Yet somehow I am here and I am speaking with you. You are a man who my family and I have always admired.

DUBE: I accept your kind words. However, I see there is work to be done for you do not have the luxury of confusion. Duty has always demanded knowledge and perspective.

MASHUDU: Baba John, please explain what you mean.

DUBE: There is a privilege to experiencing a reckoning with time, history and the land that belongs to oneself and one's ancestors. There is a privilege in being awakened. What will you do with all that is now in your hands? For you will return to the present.

MASHUDU: (*her anxiety is becoming more apparent*) I am worried I am not ready for this, I am worried I don't have the language that I need. Why was someone else not chosen? Someone who is more capable.

DUBE: (*snaps her into focus like all good teachers*) You were not chosen by accident. As I believe it was not by accident that I created the ANC. It is about purpose. The ANC had a purpose, a sense of destiny because I gave it such a destiny. You may question yourself but you may not forget you have duties as a poet. It is time I ask you a serious question.

Mashudu nods her head with caution. She is scared that she will not be able to answer right or that she might have to continue to explain the intensity of her uncertainty. She was a woman who doubted every moment of her being, every thought that grazed her forehead and every affection from another. We could say she understood the possibilities of meaning and the responsibility of truth almost too well. She knows her duty and believes in its importance but is still paralysed by her disbelief that she is the one to fulfil it. Mashudu was lost before she began this journey, trapped in a Dark Wood of the mind, which was devouring her. She had been wandering but now she is expected to have plan or at the very least a feeling of certainty about what her world meant to her. This felt impossible. It may be a privilege to experience a reckoning, but why did she have to understand what that reckoning meant immediately?

DUBE: Dante was summoned to guide you by the virtuous souls in Paradise. Why do you think you need to be shown the afterlife?

MASHUDU: I still don't understand why they chose me.

DUBE: Are you not a poet?

MASHUDU: I am attempting to be one... The truth is, I am embarrassed Baba John, for I don't know why I am here and I don't know whether I can say I am poet. I want to give you an answer but I am scared to rush it. My mother always told me the truth is always uncovered slowly. Am I allowed to call myself a poet? No one can just call themselves a poet can they? I do not want to say what is not true. I think I have to think about it more.

DUBE: It would be wise what you said, if I did not believe you knew the answer. You do not need to think about it more. You already have thoughts about this, it is now time to remember them. Remember what you know but you are too doubtful to say aloud.

Mashudu closes her eyes as she asks for her courage. We see her hand shake gently until she covers it with the other hand to hold it still. She knew what she wished to say as if she had been rehearsing it for years. However, she was of a generation where self-doubt rules supreme with many dreaming of a way out of the anxiety but never finding it. The modern disease of uncertainty and the fear of precarious footings violently raged within her. Mashudu is too young to feel safe.

MASHUDU: (*facing the audience, as if questioning them as well*) Can I be South African without knowing South Africa? I wonder because it feels as if I am faced with a puzzle and I do not know whether I am placing the picture together truthfully. I sometimes wonder whether my compulsion to understand is strange. I sometimes shout at myself, trying to tell myself to accept that things are just the way they are and that is that. But can I be South African without knowing South Africa? I am half way to somewhere and always second-guessing if I am making the right decision, not just for me but for everyone my decision could effect. I am always counting the ripples of my movements. Am I being good to the people of my country? Am I serving South Africa? I want to see with a clear eye. I want to know the wonders and ugliness of this reality without getting lost in one or the other. I want to belong but be my own. Tell me what I do when every thought is a mess. Of course it is a mess, how could it not be? South Africa is made from too many complicated patterns.

DUBE: What about your Dark Wood?

MASHUDU: (*smiling*) I am starting to think that maybe my shadows can untangle. I think it is time to return to the people I belong to.

DUBE: Do you not believe you were chosen because of what you can bring when you return to those people?

MASHUDU: Again, I don't understand what you mean.

DUBE: Do poets not return to the people they belong to reflections of themselves and the land that is theirs? Your reckoning binds you to a duty.

MASHUDU: The duty of writing?

DUBE: (*showing excitement*) Yes but write what?

MASHUDU: What is truthful.

DUBE: It is about purpose. Your purpose is to pass on and be honest about the significance of what you have learnt, understood and felt. Your purpose is to write honestly about the nature of South Africa. Let people know the shape of our country's skeleton. Let people feel the rush of blood and rhythm of breath of the South Africa they all belong to. Your purpose is to awaken.

MASHUDU: Forgive me, but how can I do this when I still don't understand the workings of Inferno? How can I awaken when I am so confused?

DUBE: To question is to awaken. Your words are already trustworthy.

MASHUDU: Baba John why all this faith?

DUBE: (*with a gentleness, his face softens*) My child, where is your faith? You still have your grandmother's wounds but there is no doubt you share the strength of her spine. You have your mother's voice and her deliberate way of being in the world. Where is your faith when they have taught you how to be?

Mashudu smiles gently to herself. It is strange being reminded of what one has always known. She can't tell John Dube that her admiration makes her doubt. Could she be as great as her mother and grandmother, since she is still finding her mind again and still walking a path that she questions? But Mashudu has never seen herself with the clear eyes that she hopes to see her reality with. She doesn't see her desire to do what's right as being a sure sign of her goodness. She doesn't see the strength of her steady defiance against the pain of the world. She doubts her resilience and questions her true brilliance and disbelieves the fact that of course she would understand the afterlife, she has always had a sense of justice. John Dube sees all that Mashudu is, so does Dante and those in Paradise. Having a partial reflection that brings in emptiness where emptiness should not be allowed, is the curse of the young. But she will untangle herself from her Dark Wood. She will visit Paradise soon enough.

Mashudu's voice grows in conviction because she now knows there will be no other way to fulfil her duty.

MASHUDU: You don't need to tell me this Uncle, I know it well. My grandmother tells me this when I visit her grave. Mr Dube I know you know my name but I want to say it out loud to you because I am proud of it.

DUBE: What is the name you must honour?

MASHUDU: My name is Mashudu, I am named after an exceptional black woman.

DUBE: Does your name keep you strong?

MASHUDU: Strong enough to write because she is close to me as I write. She makes me strong enough to fulfil my duty as a poet for my grandmother, my mother and all the black women I know and do not know.

DUBE: I then have fulfilled my own duty.

John Dube turns to Dante with a look of solemnity. Mashudu must be baptised by Purgatory so she can truly become a poet.

DUBE: You must wash her face in the water until there is no part unclean. She is true and bold and so deserves a face pure from the shadows of Inferno. We all know she is ready to know South Africa but she has been given no easy task. Don't cry child. Dante, go wipe her tears carefully from her face so she can see clearly when she writes.

Dante wipes Mashudu's tears with his sleeve and she just laughs because she is embarrassed that she is crying in front of John Dube. Yet she cannot help but be moved, which leaves her in tears as complicated as the reckoning she will turn into poetry.

DUBE: (*with a sudden burst of enthusiasm*) You were dancing before I arrived. I remember I used to dance with all my granddaughters.

MASHUDU: (*smiling*) I danced with my grandfather too. Mr Dube do you still dance?

DUBE: (*already opening his hand for Mashudu to take it*) Only on special occasions.

After John Dube takes Mashudu's hands, they come to dance the waltz. It is a calm happiness that returns to her and she is smiling and laughing at her clumsiness compared to John Dube's regal posture. Dante is smiling too and when he hears the sounds of clapping and trumpets from the Mountain he begins to laugh. The angels are waiting for Mashudu to begin to ascend. But they can wait a few more minutes. Dante can't bring himself to break her moment of beauty.

Scene IX

Purgatory Canto V and VI

The pilgrims have climbed a considerable part of the mountain yet still have not reached the Gates of Purgatory. Instead, they find themselves at the edge of a swarm of souls. They are not the souls of Inferno whose outlines are lost in shadow, these souls are unique and technicoloured. They adorn the mountain like Christmas ornaments and sparkle when the sun sweeps past them. These souls are waiting. They are caught in the hands of time. Time moves too slowly for what their hopes demand. The waiting becomes a game of trying to rid themselves of their wishes, while still doing all they can to escape the stillborn hours. All Dante and Mashudu can hear are names being spoken. The souls hope that a few more utterances of their names and the names of the loved ones who must remember them, will finally deliver them to the Gates so they can begin their ascent. The outpouring of names comes to tumble and fall off the mountain and climb up the rocks like vines. It is the murmur of prayers that create a frenzied hum in the air. Each name spoken to the stones is a prayer for closeness with the living as much as redemption. It is the call for remembrance not just to begin the ascension but to be loved enough to be saved. Whenever a soul begins the ascent a sigh ripples through the other name-speakers. They all think "I want to be loved like that."

Dante and Mashudu are standing on the edge. Dante knows how desperate the souls are for their names to be spoken by those other than themselves and so because of this is petrified they will sense their presence. He constantly pulls Mashudu back from her curiosity.

DANTE: (*whispers*) Your presence must not be known. They are trapped in the game of waiting but this cannot be our fate. They will not let you go until you speak their names aloud but you cannot do this for thousands of souls. We cannot risk being seen because we do not have time for all their names. Paradise is going to call for you soon so we cannot lose a moment on souls that will demand you to pray for their salvation.

It is the desperation for remembrance that does not let the air rest. The threat of being alone fills each soul with an unyielding anxiety. To be saved is now connected to not just the goodness of their humanity but also whether that very humanity is alive in the memories of those still living.

MASHUDU: I can hear them from here. Are they calling to their loved ones?

DANTE: Is it not both ordinary and heartbreaking to crave to be remembered? They have the same desperation they had when living— the very human desire to always be loved. Only now this desire is heightened for the saving of their souls is at stake not just their loneliness.

MASHUDU: (*leaning too far forward*) Can we not help them?

DANTE: (*Dante yanking Mashudu back*) No, you cannot let your heart buckle under their pleas. We must move along our path with fortitude as well as with the recognition of our own limitations in the face of what is required of us. Yes we can acknowledge their pain and we can move through the crowds with compassion. They are still souls that will be delivered after all. But we must accept the truth that not every sorrow has to be our own.

Before they are about to push their way into the technicolour wave of souls, they hear a soul cough behind them. Mashudu turns around and Dante shoots an exasperated sigh. The soul is sitting on the ground, he is crouched as if he deliberately made himself smaller. His head on his knees only slightly lifts when Mashudu talks to him.

MASHUDU: Are you okay sir?

Dante glares at her, this is the exact opposite of what he told her to do. The soul looks confused as if he has been woken up from a sleep that has lasted months or years. Dante gestures to Mashudu that they must leave the soul alone but she completely ignores him.

MASHUDU: Sir, can you hear me? Are you okay?

The soul is alarmed and confused. After realising that he was being asked a question, the soul peers hard at Mashudu trying to see if it really was her that spoke to him.

BUYISWA: Oh me? Are you talking to me?

MASHUDU: Yes I am. I want to know if you are okay.

BUYISWA: I am sorry. I am not used to a question like that. I thought you were asking someone else.

Mashudu tries not to show in her eyes how a needle of sadness just pierced her chest. It was such a reply of matter-of-fact anguish, that she didn't know what to do with it. She waited for him to ask her to say his name but he did not. So she decides to stay silent. He soon realises she is sincere so he coughs and begins again.

BUYISWA: I am simply waiting. I know it is going to take many more centuries, maybe even longer, before I can begin my climb. This means I have to sometimes change how I am seated and cough to clear my lungs. You just happened to be near me. This is the first time I have moved in a year.

Mashudu sits down cross-legged next to the soul, so she is not standing over him.

MASHUDU: Why aren't you calling out names like the others?

The soul spits out cynicism when he snorts and laughs. He is not resigned, he just sounds defeated.

BUYISWA: I can think of no one who loves me to make the wait go faster. I have no family and if they are still alive they certainly won't think of me. Good (*he spits*) I don't want my name anywhere near their dirty mouths. Ah these stupid souls around me who think waiting is hard. Life was hard. The afterlife is practically a holiday.

MASHUDU: Will you tell me why?

Dante gives up trying to gesture to Mashudu to be quick and sits down on a rock to listen.

BUYISWA: I was a beggar. I am sure you can picture it. I don't need to describe myself to you. (*pauses*) You were going to say sorry and then you over thought it.

MASHUDU: (*she looks away*) Yes I was. I am sorry that was rude of me.

BUYISWA: It is a sorry in many ways. But don't you take pity on me. It is one of the oldest professions in the world right? Even your ancient friend must have known a humble beggar.

MASHUDU: It must have been such a difficult existence to live. I think it would be wrong to think I could imagine or understand.

The soul pauses. He looks at them and recognises their pity, which creates the emotions he has not felt in years to thunder up to his throat. He is angered by their pity and saddened that he can still be pitied in the afterlife. He dislikes their sympathy but is still secretly happy to have someone to listen.

BUYISWA: It was difficult. What was funny was how people could know this and still not care. Many people knew how hard our life was but never wanted to see it properly. Maybe it was because they would then have to feel their own shame. Or perhaps they were scared of it. These must be the reasons that they drove past us with no sign that they saw us, or that they turned their heads after having met our eyes. No, it is not a maybe, they were scared and they felt their shame. They felt their shame that they stopped at a robot but then drove past us, they felt their shame to have met our eyes and shame to have pitied. They avoided us by looking in their laps or pretending to look for coins. Extreme poverty is not for the weak-hearted. But did they even live in it?

Mashudu shifts uncomfortably as she recognises in herself all those ways of engaging with beggars. A reckoning, here will be her shame for he is completely right.

BUYISWA: Do you know what was the worst part? It was never the hunger, it was never the cold. It was that I was always a reflection of their goodness, their cruelty or their indifference. I was painful, a nuisance, a charity case and meaningless depending on what they saw. Who I was to myself was never thought about by them. They wouldn't even care if I told them I read all the books I sold at the side of the road.

MASHUDU: I think I should feel shame for not having understood this. Shame is what I deserve.

BUYISWA: I don't know... shame can be quick and then forgotten by those with enough money. If anyone felt shame it was me.

MASHUDU: Why would you have to feel shame?

BUYISWA: I became suspicious of human kindness. Every act felt insincere. My shame was how easy it was to forget that I could be seen as a person. (*pauses*) Ah don't look at me with those teary eyes. I was no poor saint so do not pity me. I did things, that shock me still.

MASHUDU: You had to for your survival.

BUYISWA: We all own a tragedy. I just learnt that consciences serve you better in a warm bed.

DANTE: You are here in Purgatory not in Inferno. You are not damned, your soul can rise to the heavens because of your honesty.

BUYISWA: I repented in case God was real. (*laughs*) Turns out I was right. Damn that was because of Aphiwe you know? He told me to pray every night. Too bad I only started after I lost him.

MASHUDU: May I ask who was Aphiwe?

BUYISWA: My brother. (*losing his stoicism*) See I did love in my life, I knew what it meant to love another. There is something good in that.

MASHUDU: You are right, there is something good in that.

DANTE: Will you let us listen awhile longer?

Even though the soul is happy to have people listen to him and treat him with a dignity he is not known from strangers, he knows he is unearthing a pain that has not lessened but intensified as he has waited.

BUYISWA: Aphiwe was this other homeless boy. He begged on the opposite corner to me and we ended up becoming friends. Mostly because he wouldn't leave me alone. He was much younger than me, orphaned by a drinker-father like many of us left out in the open. Soon I decided we would stick together. Perhaps it was because of loneliness but that is too simple. Once we got speaking we just couldn't stop. There was a homeless shelter near to our corners but you needed a set amount of money to enter. Whenever he couldn't make it because no one was kind enough that day, I would give him some of my money if I had won the pity lottery. He always protested but I would say firmly that it couldn't be any different and so he would give in. If we both couldn't get enough money we would sleep next to each other.

The soul begins to cry, Mashudu moves to grab his hand.

BUYISWA: One day Aphiwe just did not come back. I walked the whole city looking for him. I waited for him, watched out for him and every moment I was alive I thought of him. So when I came here I understood he must be on his way to Paradise by now as he had someone that loved him keeping him in their thoughts. He always had me. He always had me saying his name. And so who loves me? No one. So I am waiting. Luckily the afterlife is eternal and waiting a thousand years doesn't stop me from being united with Aphiwe again. He was my brother. He is my brother. We always said we would be brothers forever. I haven't ever stopped believing that to be true.

Dante knows what Mashudu is going to do. He smiles to encourage her for he now knows that it was the work of divine justice for her to meet this soul. Never before had Mashudu truly understood the term— the human condition. She couldn't imagine this soul's life on the streets though she could recognise the horror of her own causal cruelty to people like him. She could understand how he loved for she loved her sister like it. She could understand his sorrow because she had felt the darkness trap itself like a million-year grief inside of her. So she held his hand and he held hers. There was not a sense of complete understanding between them but there was at least something beautiful— the beginning of a caring acknowledgement.

MASHUDU: (*with a gentle excitement*) I am still of the living so I will keep you in my thoughts. Hopefully, this will allow you to be closer to reuniting with Aphiwe. What is your name?

BUYISWA: Buyiswa, my name is Buyiswa. (*pauses with a tremor in his voice*) Did you know I almost forgot it? I almost forgot my name. (*pauses*) What is your name?

MASHUDU: My name is Mashudu.

BUYISWA: Mashudu please think of me. I miss my brother more than anything. I don't want Paradise to be so far away from me because I can't bear the distance between me and my brother. I want to be closer. I need Aphiwe to be close.

Virgil comes onto the stage but this time holds himself seriously. What he is about to say deserves a kind of respect.

VIRGIL: A poet has language and a poet has the power to remember. Some write to remember the stories of lands, time, of the epic and the greats. Homer, Dante and I, we all had the ego and the desire of constructing history. Mashudu in her own way will carve out the history of South Africa and lead others to the present. But Mashudu is also more than us three, she writes to remember for a different kind of greatness. Mashudu writes to remember in order to be kind. She never forgot about her promise to Buyiswa all her life. She would write his name many times a day. One day, feeling him too far away, she decided to write him a letter.

Virgil takes out a letter and reads it.

"Buyiswa, I found you waiting. You were held closely by the sadness of too many years passing. But now I write your name out as beautifully as I can and write you letters as if we knew each other's faces for a lifetime instead of a moment. I write your name so that the waiting doesn't hurt your lungs or make you cry. I want you to know that the wait will never be meaningless because soon you will feel the closeness of love returned to you. You will have your brother stand right there instead of in a dream. Buyiswa I found you waiting so I say your name. Buyiswa, you are remembered. Buyiswa I will say your brother's name too."

Scene X

Purgatory Canto XIII

There is a mystical beauty that settles on the Mountain of Purgatory. The audience watches how the Mountain glimmers in the sunlight. Mashudu tries to remind herself of this magnificence when her lungs are protesting as she climbs. Mashudu runs her hands across the cliff edges. The coldness of the satin stone calms her. Her mind surges like electricity without wires. How could she capture what she has seen? How could she capture the emotions that spill through her like paint? Mashudu wonders if she has reached the point of her having had too much experience. She wonders whether her travels in the afterlife have been too vivid for too long. That she was supposed to come and eventually leave to return to the present much earlier. But here she is, walking up the Mountain with her legs on fire. She knows she must embrace the vividness and find solace in the intensity. The afterlife was never going to be an easy road. But, as she has come to understand, neither would have been staying in the Dark Wood.

However, this sense of peace within her is short lived for she soon reaches the terrace of envy and sees the souls earning their salvation. Penance must have been woven into their sackcloth clothes. The souls lean against the mountain and each other. It is a kind and desperate solidarity. Mashudu, when seeing that their eyes were closed, thought that the souls were merely tired. She believed she was just seeing the exhaustion of redemption's work. She had half a mind to sit next to them and close her eyes as well. Instead, Dante motions for her to go closer so she can see their eyes properly. Mashudu goes slowly as if trying not to wake them before she recognises that the souls' eyes have been sewn shut with wire. They were all weeping but their tears took so long to fall beyond the stitches that by the time they ran down their cheeks, the souls were crying crystals.

MASHUDU: Dante all their eyes are closed. Are they praying?

DANTE: "Each one rests his head upon the other// In order to arouse our pity quickly// Not merely by the sound of what they say// But by the sight which cries out just as loudly// And like the blind, neglected by the sun// So the shades here which I am speaking of// Find heaven's light is nowhere to be seen// For their eyelids are threaded through and sewn// With iron wire like savage sparrow hawks.// Treated that way to help make them tame." (63-72)

MASHUDU: (*in a state that is a mixture of curiosity and shock*) Their eyes... They have been turned blind.

But why? Where are we?

DANTE: We have arrived at the terrace of envy.

MASHUDU: So why are their eyes sewn shut?

DANTE: Here we have sinners who could not stop themselves gazing. Gazing at others, gazing with the intent of choosing facts of life that should have been theirs. They watched in order to fuel their ritual of counting who possesses and who lacks. Jealousy makes the eyes obsessive.

Mashudu comes to a woman in front of her with eyes imprisoned by crystal tears. She hopes to relieve her of her discomfort even though she knows this is probably not allowed by divine justice. Mashudu doesn't know that divine justice requires her to recognise this soul. That the fate of the afterlife has been positioning her kindness without her knowing.

MASHUDU: (*addressing the soul, timidly*) Would it help you if I remove some of your tears?

SINAZO: I would like that a lot. My hardened tears tug at this wire that has closed my eyes. I know I don't have eyelashes anymore.

Mashudu recognises the woman and steps back in fright. Her head motions her mind trying to remove her disbelief. It is Sinazo, a lost childhood friend who had disappeared into other schools and neighbourhoods. Mashudu recognised her despite all the years.

Fate was always going to call forth her memories ensuring that an instant wave of guilt threatened to make her unravel. She had not thought of Sinazo for years.

MASHUDU: (*coming closer again*) Sinazo is that you? I don't know if you will remember me, it is Mashudu. My heart breaks knowing you have died.

SINAZO: (*her head moves aggressively*) Mashudu? Yes I do remember. I remember a lot but it has been so many years, let us not count them. Why are you sorry I have died? I am not sorry so I don't need you to be sad, especially since your sadness has only conveniently come now, instead of when it mattered most. When did you die?

Mashudu begins to detect the bite in how Sinazo speaks to her.

MASHUDU: Would you believe it if I told you I wasn't dead? I am being guided through the afterlife. I am just a visitor for now. I just hope I remain living so I can get back.

SINAZO: (*sneering*) Of course it would be you that was chosen to be alive and in the afterlife. Some of us had to go the conventional route but you have always been spectacular. Isn't that true?

MASHUDU: (*earnestly*) I do believe I was meant to see you again.

SINAZO: Oh really? I am so lucky.

MASHUDU: Can you tell me why your eyes are sewn shut?

SINAZO: Are you jealous?

Mashudu can feel the simmering anger that turns all of Sinazo's words hot, quick and aggressive. Although, Sinazo cannot hide that her sarcasm is tempered with moments of great melancholy, as if her bones are being shattered underneath her own ferocity. Mashudu knows she shouldn't feel as disorientated as she is, listening to Sinazo's words of anger. She knows she should have thought of Sinazo a long time ago.

SINAZO: I know that I saved myself through asking God for forgiveness. A death bed does put things into perspective, even though meeting a person from the past in the afterlife can threaten to undo all that. (*with great melancholy*) I personally like to believe that God let my eyes close so I can just have a break from it all. But maybe it is always easier for broken people to believe they are touched with care.

MASHUDU: You don't have to tell me if you don't want to. I just want to understand.

SINAZO: (*her head snaps back to being aggressive*) Ah Miss Bright Light wants to finally understand. Wow, I have rehearsed this in my mind for you and all your friends for so long. Take the message to them when you return all famous. We all used to be friends remember? I guess circumstances are always thicker than friendship.

MASHUDU: I missed something before, I don't want to miss it again.

SINAZO: Oh you missed things? Yes, you did miss things. Our worlds got separated as soon as my father started filling his whiskey glass up to the rim with no ice. You never will understand the meaning of an empty bottle. Oh your father with his two glasses of whiskey a week that your mother still scolded him for. What a terrible life you lived. It must have been so sad for you to never have to dodge the cigarettes aimed directly at your eyes. A missing experience for a writer don't you think? We could never have been close. (*her voice almost breaking before it turns back to rage*) I had the father who shouted curses at me and touched me wrongly. You had the father that hugged you. This is why I believe God has closed my eyes. I cannot take the suffering of my memories.

MASHUDU: I didn't know I missed so much.

SINAZO: Stop lying Mashudu, we are too deep into the afterlife for that. You missed things? Was it really not deliberate? Let me give you the benefit of the doubt and you really did miss the sad details of my life. But missed meanings did not mean you did not know something was wrong. It was the worst kept secret in the school, the fact of me and my mother's shame.

MASHUDU: My mother just told me I couldn't come to your house, you could only come to mine.

SINAZO: That means you knew. Adults really do have a talent for never intervening. I was jealous of your strong willed mother compared to my mother, all skeletal and withering away. But I guess even the strong-willed were not strong enough to help me. I was so jealous of your selfish family, your stupid, selfish perfect family. You knew, you all knew and it only got worse.

MASHUDU: I remember you left school.

SINAZO: Ah all the fake goodbyes. I had to leave. Drunken taxes cannot buy private school luxury. How was university? Must be nice to be clever and educated. I am sure university has led you here Miss Bright Light.

MASHUDU: I found Dante in university.

SINAZO: And that is why you are here. Maybe I would be dragged through the afterlife if I had time to read.

MASHUDU: It is more than that.

SINAZO: I envied you all so much that I almost hated you. It was so unfair. You private school babies and you especially Miss Bright Light, so pretty, so brilliant, so free. (*with desperation*) And what about me? Why did you abandon me? Where I had to look at you and always know what I could never have?

Mashudu looks as if her past has fractured. She isn't even crying but her hands violently shake. She has bitten her lip so hard it bleeds. She mumbles her apologies over and over again as if they are her own prayer for redemption.

MASHUDU: (*quietly and painfully*) I am so sorry Sinazo. I am so sorry.

SINAZO: Are you sorry? Where were you though?

MASHUDU: (*louder with more urgency*) I am sorry. I am sorry.

SINAZO: No one reached out towards me, no one cared because I was on the wrong side of things. I had a nothing mother and a father who loved gin more than he loved me. I remember your parents, I remember our school. You were loved and I was forgotten. Left to care for my father who made himself sick from the rum.

MASHUDU: Sinazo...

SINAZO: Before you say one more word, I don't want to hear how sorry you are again. I don't want your guilt and I certainly don't want to hear any excuses that you were young and didn't understand. I envied you and look my eyes are sewn shut and I am dead, while you are still living but get chosen to waltz through the afterlife.

MASHUDU: Sinazo....

SINAZO: (*slowed down, honest and dejected*) It is time for you to go. I am so scared God has heard my anger and spite and so divine justice will take me away from Purgatory. I gave up my repentance in showing my anger to you. I have been shattered and I may be used to devastation, but I really need to be saved. I need to have my soul reach peace. I am hurting. It is not just my eyes but everything. It all just hurts. I have been in pain for so long. I have been in pain from the beginning. But you have ruined my penances and now my redemption is so far away again. Go because you've given me more decades with my eyes sewn shut. Go, before you take more away from me.

Mashudu walks away and Dante follows her. She still cannot cry but yet her body crumples and she collapses onto the ground. She holds her stomach and rocks back and forth. She had been constantly wrestling with the morals of others on her travels. She was looking at divine justice as something delivered to the dead but didn't think of what box of fate she would open in the afterlife herself. Her reckoning was not just about the South African reality that was beyond her, it was also where she found herself in the picture. Before Mashudu can go to Paradise, she has come to know that she is not a being of Paradise. It is a premonition for, like Dante, she is still a creature of Purgatory.

Dante sits down on the floor next to her and she leans into him. They are true friends now and so Dante has earned the right to comfort her.

MASHUDU: What can I say to you Dante? You have now heard my shame, a shame I didn't even recognise. This makes me so wrong. I have caused so much pain, I hurt her so deeply and left her completely alone.

DANTE: You were so young and you are still young now. The burden is not on your shoulders. The pain of being young is in our imperfections.

MASHUDU: I cannot hide behind being young can I? What is wrong is wrong. I was selfish, I was negligent and uncaring. And I thought I was the one suffering? I feel sick. I don't know what to do with this. Dante, I always saw her as a memory never as a person.

DANTE: I have made these mistakes. Sometimes what we cannot see has consequences and devastating ones. Our regrets will always be our own. But is this the whole truth of this story? Is there not more to these mistakes than shame?

MASHUDU: Not when those regrets are unredeemable.

DANTE: Do you believe you are unredeemable?

MASHUDU: I finally understand the difference between those in Purgatory and those in Inferno. There are those that are aware of the harm they cause and those who are not. I am too close to Inferno. I can feel the fire again and my eyes see the Devil. (*she begins rocking again*) I am too close to Inferno because I didn't know the whole truth or maybe because I looked away so I wouldn't have to deal with the whole truth. I showed no remorse because I didn't recognise what I did was wrong. How could I have been so careless?

DANTE: Divine justice is not about a blame that has no nuance or intricacy. It is almost too complicated to be a person and justice understands this. We dream of wisdom but when we are young no one knows what it is or what it means. And then we grow older and our complications grow with us, so wisdom becomes even more elusive.

MASHUDU: I can't fix it though. Nothing can change.

Dante rises and begins to pull Mashudu up. He wipes her tears like he did when John Dube asked him to and holds her shoulders.

DANTE: You are not a being of the afterlife, justice has not yet determined your fate. So let us not wallow in a regret that binds us to passivity. You are living still, you must not take this lightly. What has happened is tragic but you are a woman with a future. So, where do you go from here?

MASHUDU: I don't know.

DANTE: (*sterner*) That is not an answer. Where do you go from here?

Mashudu breathes in to call for her courage. She tells herself that she is living, that her actions still count. Is this not the purpose of a reckoning? It is the knowledge that one has been brought closer to the world to act in it. Mashudu has been brought closer to the truth of her reality. It is a reality that includes every bit of her complexities. For Mashudu now understands, resignation would simply be an insult to the divine.

MASHUDU: I will continue to ascend the Mountain.

DANTE: Why?

MASHUDU: Because I will not be purified sitting here, collapsed on these rocks. Although it is hard to call for redemption, I will not let myself be paralysed and numb.

DANTE: You are not of Purgatory yet. You are still of the living. So Mashudu, my poet and my friend— how will you be good?

MASHUDU: I will be honest.

Mashudu gives Dante a hug and then grabs his shoulders and looks at him with a new found boldness.

MASHUDU: I will write.

She walks on and Dante shakes his head and smiles. It is a smile of loss for he knows he belongs to Purgatory and so he cannot leave the mountain.

Scene XI

Purgatory Canto XXVII

Dante and Mashudu can both sense an ending and so they walk on in silence. Their shoulders occasionally bump into each other for the comfort of each other's presence. Both are waiting for the other to speak but are frightened that those words will be the last. Unlikely friendships are what hold the possibility of humanity together. What else can explain the phenomenon of a medieval man from Florence and a black South African woman becoming friends? They had earned the right to know each other. But unlikely friendships sadly also have the greater threat of partings and are always dropped into endings unexpectedly. In essence, unlikely friendships are unpredictable. For our two pilgrims they are coming to an understanding that if they are to see each other again both time and divine justice has to collide perfectly once more. A goodbye for Mashudu never felt greater than this one and for Dante he feels the loss so acutely he is scared to look at her or he will cry. The only hope they have is that they are both poets. The uncanny always happens to poets, it is the risk that they have always taken. Hope has not yet been lost even if Mashudu cannot hear its whispers. She will continue to write letters to the unknown, hoping Dante will know they are meant for him, her dearest friend.

Our pilgrims walk in a forest but unlike the Dark Wood, this is a forest of light. The theatre is shining with a golden glow as if the summer sun had turned herself kind. The light is not harsh like the sunlight of noon. Its clarity gives way to haziness as it is the sunlight of transformations. It can only belong to the place just before somewhere and just after somewhere else. The sun won't turn away yet. It is waiting for the pilgrims to say goodbye.

Virgil breaks the world for a moment as he holds an air of solemnity. Virgil is the first sign to the audience that this awakened stillness will soon move on without them.

VIRGIL: Memories can feel so alive for the dead. My nostalgia cannot be contained as I remember my own journey those 700 years ago. I was much older and wiser then. But despite the emergence of my youth, I still know endings well. Our pilgrims know it is time. The sunlight is enough to trigger a sense of an ending as it has just begun to set. The day is closing, it is time to let go.

Dante wants to be unsure that this is the time he will say those lines that will send Mashudu to Paradise. But he is certain and so his heart inevitably breaks. He places a hand on Mashudu's shoulder so she can stop walking. She is about to say something but before she can, she recognises an expression of sorrow so filled with love it can only be called beautiful. She knows his words are coming, she knows she is not ready to say goodbye. The sun continues to set.

VIRGIL: (*sniffling*) Oh Dante I know what you are going to say because it is exactly what I said to you. It will break your heart but you have to say it.

Virgil says the words to us for they are private between Dante and Mashudu. By his last line the sun has finally set.

VIRGIL: "Expect no further word or sign from me//Your will is now upright and free and proper// Did you not follow it, you'd go astray." (139-141) She looks as confused as he was. She doesn't understand that he is a man of Purgatory. She doesn't believe this is an ending. She won't let herself believe it is an ending. But it has to be, it always has to be.

An explosion of light shines through the space and we hear Mashudu's name being called by many voices. One voice sounds the clearest, a woman with a voice like rain. Mashudu walks slowly to the melody and the light. She knows it is time for her to go. As she is transfixed by what is in front of her, Dante slips quietly away. She moves because she believes he is close, she feels safe because she thought he was behind her. Just as she is about to go into the light she turns as if wanting to say something but can't see Dante. A forced recognition comes upon her as she feels the emptiness next to her. Her companion had said goodbye for the both of them.

MASHUDU: (*she turns around, panicked*) Dante? Dante where are you? I have been called to Paradise. Lillian Ngoyi is calling me. You were right, the virtuous souls want me to meet them. They all calling for me Dante so I am calling for you. Lillian won't wait so where are you? I want you to meet them with me.

Mashudu hears the voice calling again. She wipes the tears from her eyes and turns to the light. She wished she could have waited more but knew that he was gone before she realised it. She wished he saw her into the light, so she could tell him she was confused again because she was so scared and happy. But she knew it must have been sad to watch her go and that his heart must be hurting too. Just before she walks into the glow she shouts at the top of her voice.

MASHUDU: Goodbye Dante... Thank you for everything.

She walks into the light and is gone. The sound of the forest dies down and the chatter of a cafe emerges from the wings. Two play technicians come onto the stage with a table and two chairs. Virgil is showing them where to place the furniture. He then sits down and starts crying before taking out a pack of tissues and blowing his nose.

VIRGIL: What? I am a poet. I am plagued by emotions, haunted by emotions. Don't let my cool facade fool you, nothing hurts me more than the goodbye of friends that still love each other. This ending, like all the endings, summoned a beginning. But that is a different story that Mashudu will have to tell you in her own words. What I can say is that Mashudu did indeed come to write about this ending when documenting her travels. I think she won't mind that I read something small to you, even though I don't feel put together at all. Poets are emotional creatures, you must understand. We are better left alone in times like this but I am sure you want closure. I need closure too. So let me begin:

"The white light that burned me clean could never have cleansed me of that goodbye. All that I ever needed to say to him rushed to my lips only to evaporate in this now bright absence. I turned into the white light that burned me pure and said thank you again and again. All I hoped for was that my friend was close enough to hear it and if he was not, that the angels would take my gratitude to wherever he found himself on that great mountain."

Virgil takes a tissue and blows his nose again. He lights a cigarette, orders a beer from a waiter and then looks at his watch. The beer arrives, Virgil lights another cigarette and then looks up at the audience with a smirk. He knew they had no choice but to wait for him.

VIRGIL: Are you seriously still here? Did you honestly expect to go with her to Paradise? Listen, I know it is a tough truth but we just don't all get divine sanction or grace. We have to live vicariously through Mashudu's words, when they arrive complete after she has been ready to write them. Great art, great truths and great reckonings require slowly created masterpieces. I know, it is a bitter pill to swallow when we are so used to Tik Tok videos with their pseudo-entertainment and Instagram stories with their pseudo-authenticity. Let us stay here and try not to follow. This is the curse of those that happen to be pagan or who happen not to be poets.

Dante walks in and sits next to Virgil. He finishes Virgil's beer and so another is quickly ordered. Dante then lights a cigarette as well.

VIRGIL: Dante! Howzit my bru.

DANTE: What tongue are you speaking Virgil?

VIRGIL: You say aweh ma se kind back to me.

Dante stares awkwardly at the audience.

VIRGIL: (*speeding up as he speaks*) I can't learn a language in the span of a theatre production but I can twist myself South African. The Greeks have told me I have gotten boring in more ways than one, so I had to spice it up. Eish my bra we can't say the same things over the same Black Labels for eternity without being killed by the dwaal. I say we get a box for the next bokke game. The biltong will be on me because I don't like it too fatty. We will have to find good vetkoek and bunny chow as well and we have to go to Soweto. You must decide before if you a chief or a pirate okay? Whichever one you choose it will be messy like those scrums! (*pauses to breathe*) See, Dante I was always a boet I just never realised. And you my bru are my boitjie.

DANTE: You pagan. (*shakes his head and laughs*) What did you do Virgil?

VIRGIL: (*gesturing at the audience*) Some kind person in the audience lent me their phone and I searched how to speak like a South African.

DANTE: Well I have no South African to speak to anymore.

Virgil places his hand on Dante's hand and then lights another cigarette for him.

VIRGIL: So how was it to be a guide on a pilgrimage? How was it to see another's fate unravel like a thread?

DANTE: I don't know. I am completely overcome.

VIRGIL: You can do better than that. You do know.

DANTE: I think there is a kind of divinity in the journey when a poet leads a poet. There will always be divinity in the act of guiding a person out of the Dark Wood.

VIRGIL: Just like I guided you.

DANTE: Yes, just like you guided me. (*sits back in the chair and collapses*) Even though it is exhausting.

VIRGIL: You a little unfit hey Dante?

DANTE: Tell me, who is fit enough to hear Minos and his cattle teeth?

VIRGIL: (*playfully hitting Dante*) You have to practice self-care Dante. I have been telling you this.

DANTE: Even then, I could only do this every 700 years.

VIRGIL: (*nearly knocking over the beer*) Wait, you want to do this again?

DANTE: Of course because I will have Mashudu besides me. Her poems will survive the centuries as ours have.

VIRGIL: Oh yes, we will have her. Pity you never introduced me.

DANTE: She had to go to Paradise and you were out here on a rampage with some poor audience member's phone.

VIRGIL: Can't argue with that, can I? (*with too much excitement*) I think we should all be guides together to completely overwhelm the poet who comes next. Think about it, we all have our different vibes. You boring, she's great and I am the sassy flavouring on everyone's chip n dip.

DANTE: Is this a good idea? Virgil I do question what **Limbo** is doing to your mind.

VIRGIL: I know, it is all the philosophers down there... But, listen Dante, a poet can handle anything. Look at you! Look at her! Look at me!

DANTE: I have pondered what I can do when Mashudu and I reunite. Something that could be a surprise. Show her that the next journey is not the afterlife but South Africa itself.

VIRGIL: (*smiling kindly*) Let us start small.

DANTE: What do you mean?

VIRGIL: Say something in the South African tongue.

DANTE: There are so many languages to learn.

VIRGIL: Eleven languages to be exact. Dante, never mind that, we can start even smaller, tinier. Say shap-shap.

DANTE: Shap-shap Virgil, this was all shap-shap.

Excerpts of Inferno and Purgatory translated by J.G Nichols

Bibliography

Alighieri, D. 1320. *The Divine Comedy: Inferno*. Trans. J.G Nichols. 2010. Surrey, UK: Alma Classics.

Alighieri, D. 1320. *The Divine Comedy: Purgatory*. Trans. J.G Nichols. 2011. Surrey, UK: Alma Classics.

Acknowledgements

I have always been told that being a writer is a solitary job. In many senses that could be said to be true. Yet as I began to write these acknowledgements I realised how many people embraced the process of the writing of this play with me, as well as all the people I met along the way. A Long Walk to Purgatory has been a path that has shown me the beauty of my community. So as you begin to read these acknowledgements, let these votes of thanks acknowledge how the act of creating art is a path that may in times be solitary, but is never lonely.

First and foremost, I must thank Dr Anita Virga, head of the Dante Alighieri Society. Thank you for seeing me as a writer with potential as well as trusting me with the idea of adapting Dante to the South African context for the Dante Alighieri Society. I am so appreciative of all your support, kindness and faith in my writing. I am so grateful for your guidance. You not only extended to me such an immense opportunity but also opened up my mind to new creative pathways and a deeper, more enriching relationship with Dante. It has truly been a great honour to be supported by the Italian institutions of South Africa such as the Dante Alighieri Society in Johannesburg, the Embassy of Italy in Pretoria, the Consulate General of Italy in Johannesburg, the Consulate General of Italy in Cape Town and the Italian Cultural Institute in Pretoria. Your culture has been an enormous inspiration to me, thank you so much for giving me the opportunity to express this. This all would not have happened without the Dantessa Society at Wits, my home. Thank you Dr Sonia Fanucchi for your warmth and feedback on all my writing, not only a Long Walk to Purgatory.

To the thespians who are making this possible. I want to start with those I knew from the very beginning — Lerato Sefoloshe, our Mashudu and Mlindeli Zondi, our director— I am so grateful to you both for your guidance, generosity and kindness. I remember that day of sitting around the table with my rough draft (we will not call it a first) with Alessandro

Parodi, Benedetta Coli and Dr Anita Virga. That day of imagining together what this could be gave me the confidence to really begin the writing process.

To the Johannesburg School of Mask and Movement (JMAM) team. I cannot wait to see what happens when the writing is in your hands. Thank you to Kyla Davis, Roberto Pombo, Daniel Buckland (our Dante), Nokuthula Mabuza and Walter Goqo. I am so excited for the words on the page to become the masked characters on stage. Even though Devon Du Plessis is my good friend and technically not a thespian per se, he deserves to be included here because I would not have managed the scene of South African slang without my "boitjie".

To my dearest family and to my dearest friends who are family. What words are there when I do not know how to truly encompass the gratitude I feel for all of you? You have never once told me to stop talking, and never once stopped listening, when I spoke endlessly about the trials and tribulations of writing, or the frightening feelings of admin Inferno (I know this must have been tough because I have a tendency to harp on about things). You have all encouraged me, supported me and reminded me to have faith in myself. Please know, that with every word you read, it was all because of you. It was because of the snippets you read when I sent them to you at strange hours, it was because of me bombarding you with the scenes I was writing when you were at my house or on phone calls. I cannot believe you let me ramble on and yet you did it with such kindness. You know who you are and you know how much I love you. I am so immensely grateful that you walked this path with me. Dante may be Mashudu's Virgil, but you are all my Virgil. You have been the ones that have guided me through the Commedia of writing a Long Walk to Purgatory. Once more we look upon the stars my loves.

And finally to my darling Dante. Thank you for your words, your Cantos, your worlds of the afterlife. You have been my Beatrice, my ultimate Muse. I will not make it to Paradise, I am a Purgatory kinda gal. This is good news, for I will eventually see you there on that mountain. However, until then, I will revisit your writings again and again.